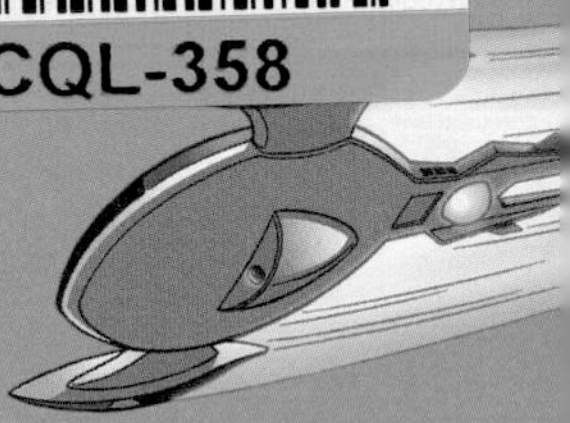

GREEN LANTERN
THE ANIMATED SERIES™

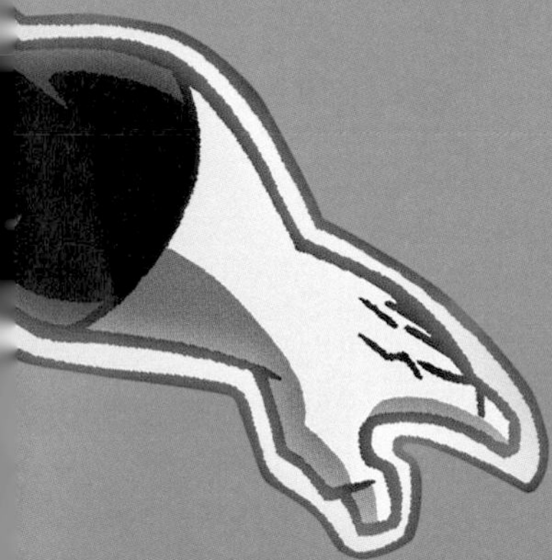

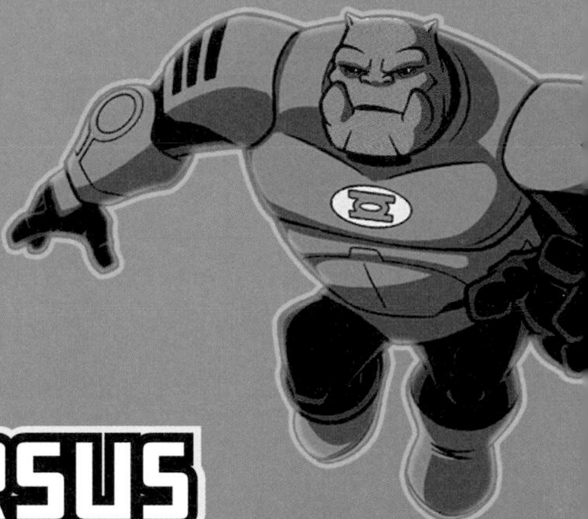

HAL VERSUS ATROCITUS

Art Baltazar & Franco....................writers
Dario Brizuela............................ illustrator
Gabe Eltaeb ....colorist
Saida Temofonte ....letterer

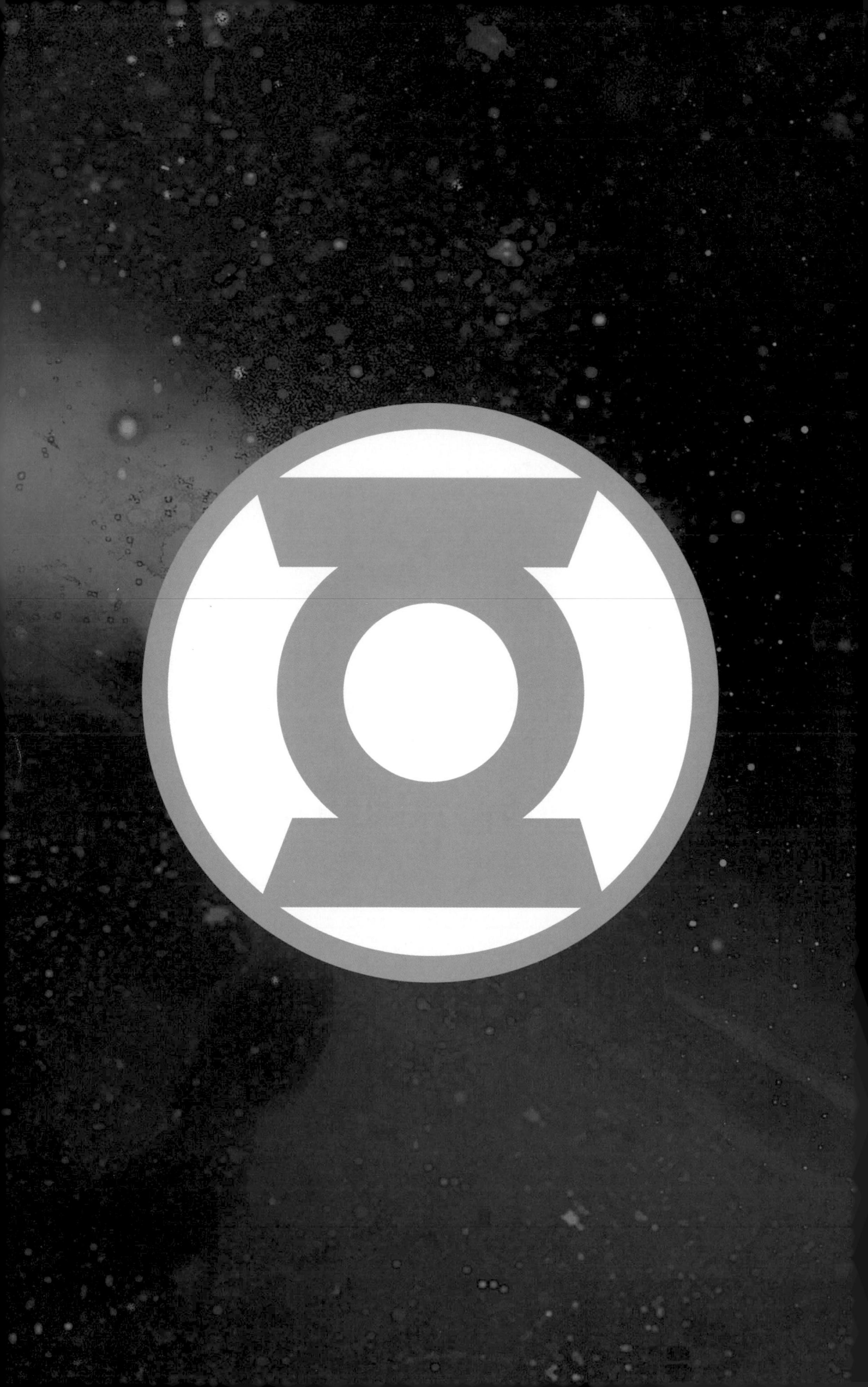

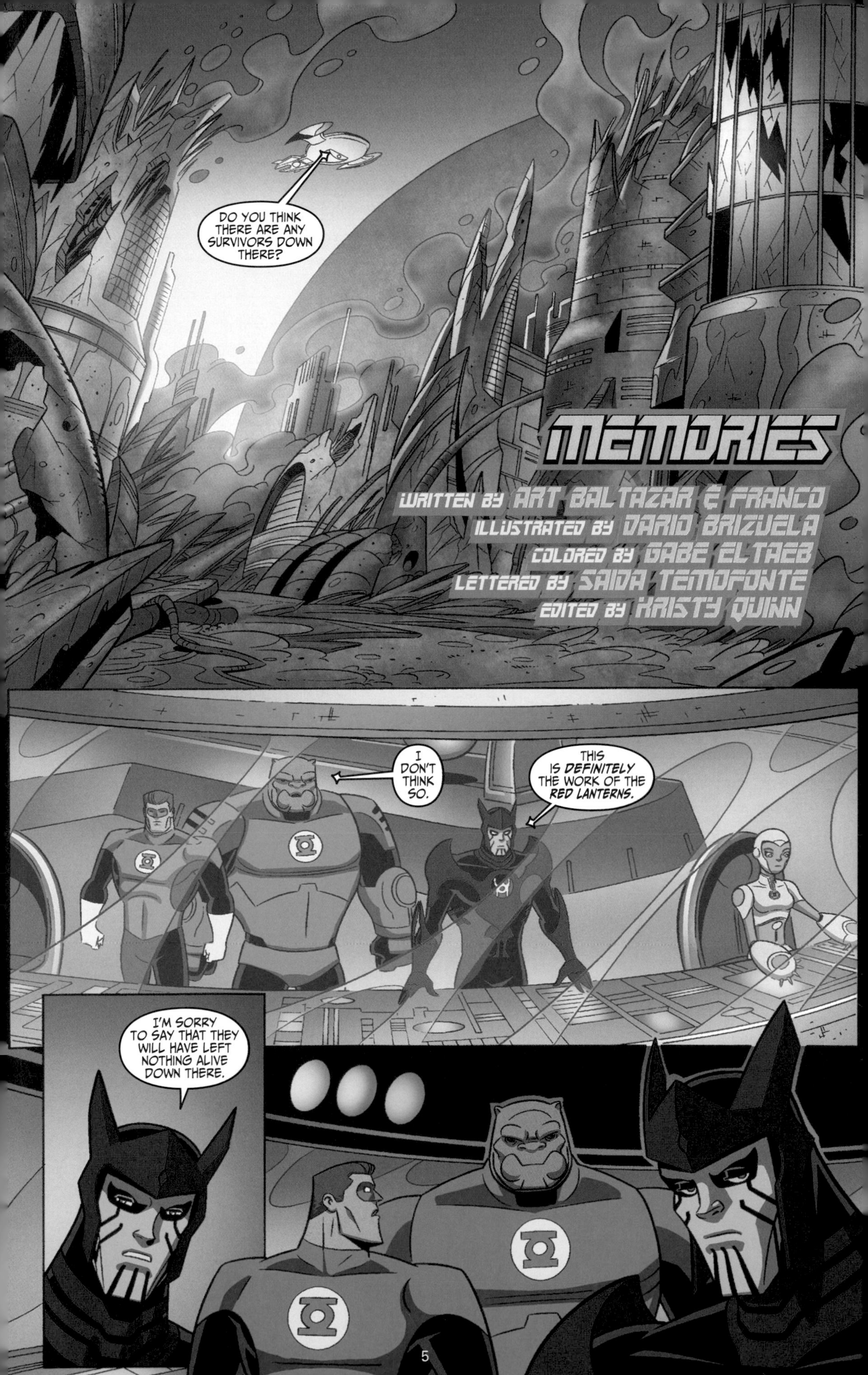
DO YOU THINK THERE ARE ANY SURVIVORS DOWN THERE?
MEMORIES
WRITTEN BY ART BALTAZAR & FRANCO
ILLUSTRATED BY DARIO BRIZUELA
COLORED BY GABE ELTAEB
LETTERED BY SAIDA TEMOFONTE
EDITED BY KRISTY QUINN
I DON'T THINK SO.
THIS IS DEFINITELY THE WORK OF THE RED LANTERNS.
I'M SORRY TO SAY THAT THEY WILL HAVE LEFT NOTHING ALIVE DOWN THERE.

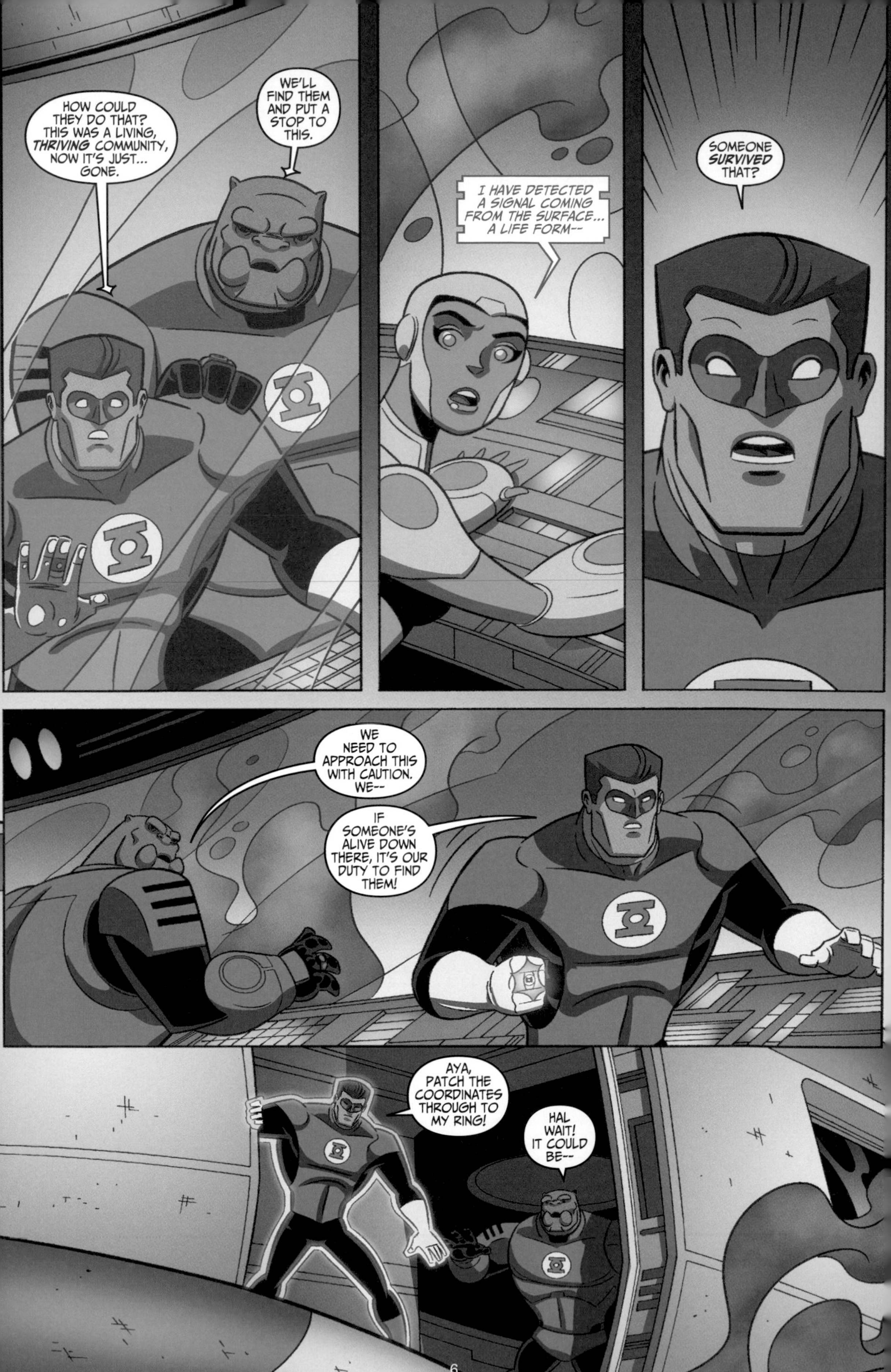
HOW COULD THEY DO THAT? THIS WAS A LIVING, THRIVING COMMUNITY, NOW IT'S JUST... GONE.
WE'LL FIND THEM AND PUT A STOP TO THIS.
I HAVE DETECTED A SIGNAL COMING FROM THE SURFACE... A LIFE FORM--
SOMEONE SURVIVED THAT?
WE NEED TO APPROACH THIS WITH CAUTION. WE--
IF SOMEONE'S ALIVE DOWN THERE, IT'S OUR DUTY TO FIND THEM!
AYA, PATCH THE COORDINATES THROUGH TO MY RING!
HAL WAIT! IT COULD BE--

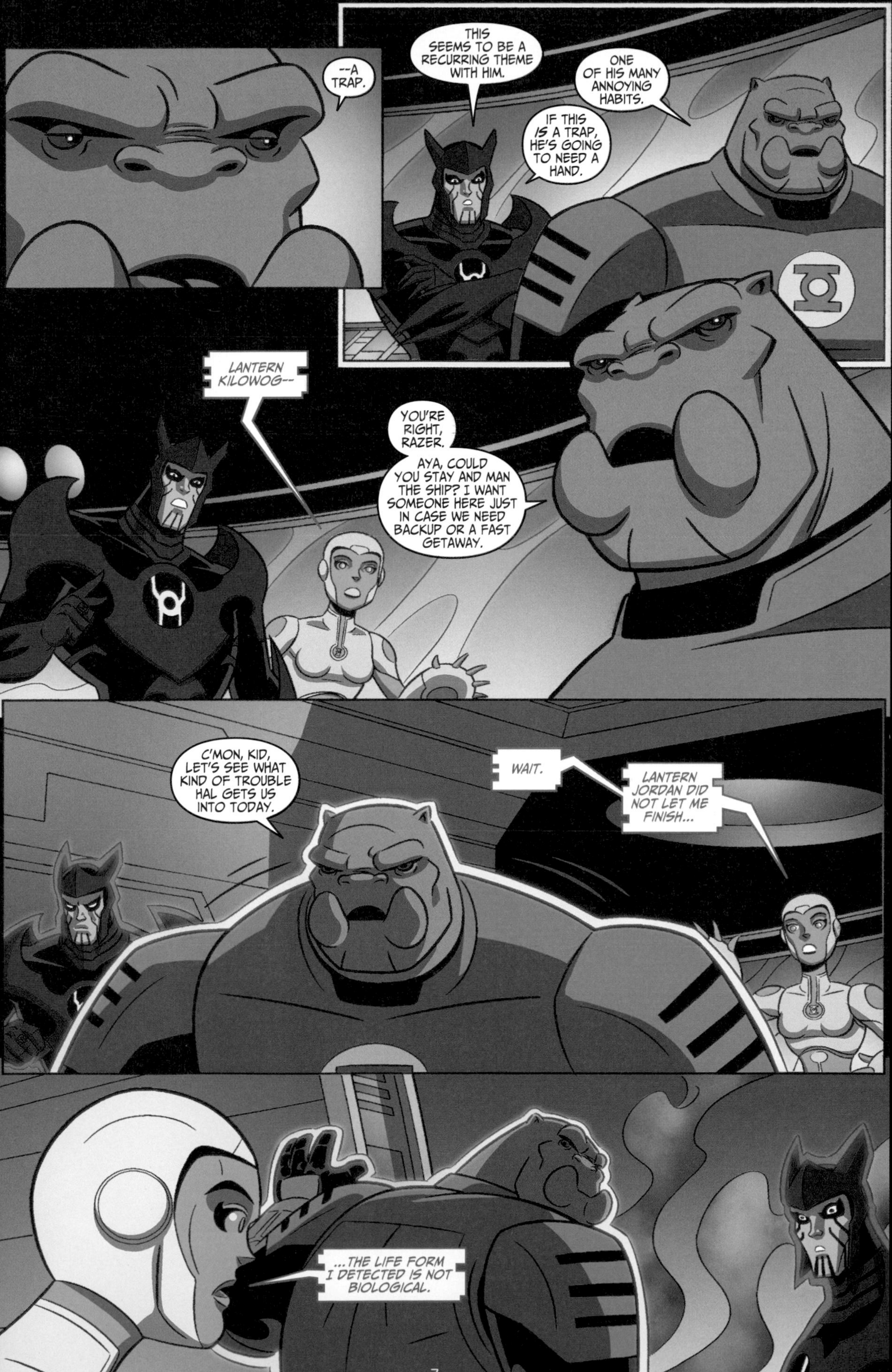
--A TRAP.
THIS SEEMS TO BE A RECURRING THEME WITH HIM.
ONE OF HIS MANY ANNOYING HABITS.
IF THIS *IS* A TRAP, HE'S GOING TO NEED A HAND.
LANTERN KILOWOG--
YOU'RE RIGHT, RAZER.
AYA, COULD YOU STAY AND MAN THE SHIP? I WANT SOMEONE HERE JUST IN CASE WE NEED BACKUP OR A FAST GETAWAY.
C'MON, KID, LET'S SEE WHAT KIND OF TROUBLE HAL GETS US INTO TODAY.
WAIT.
LANTERN JORDAN DID NOT LET ME FINISH...
...THE LIFE FORM I DETECTED IS NOT BIOLOGICAL.

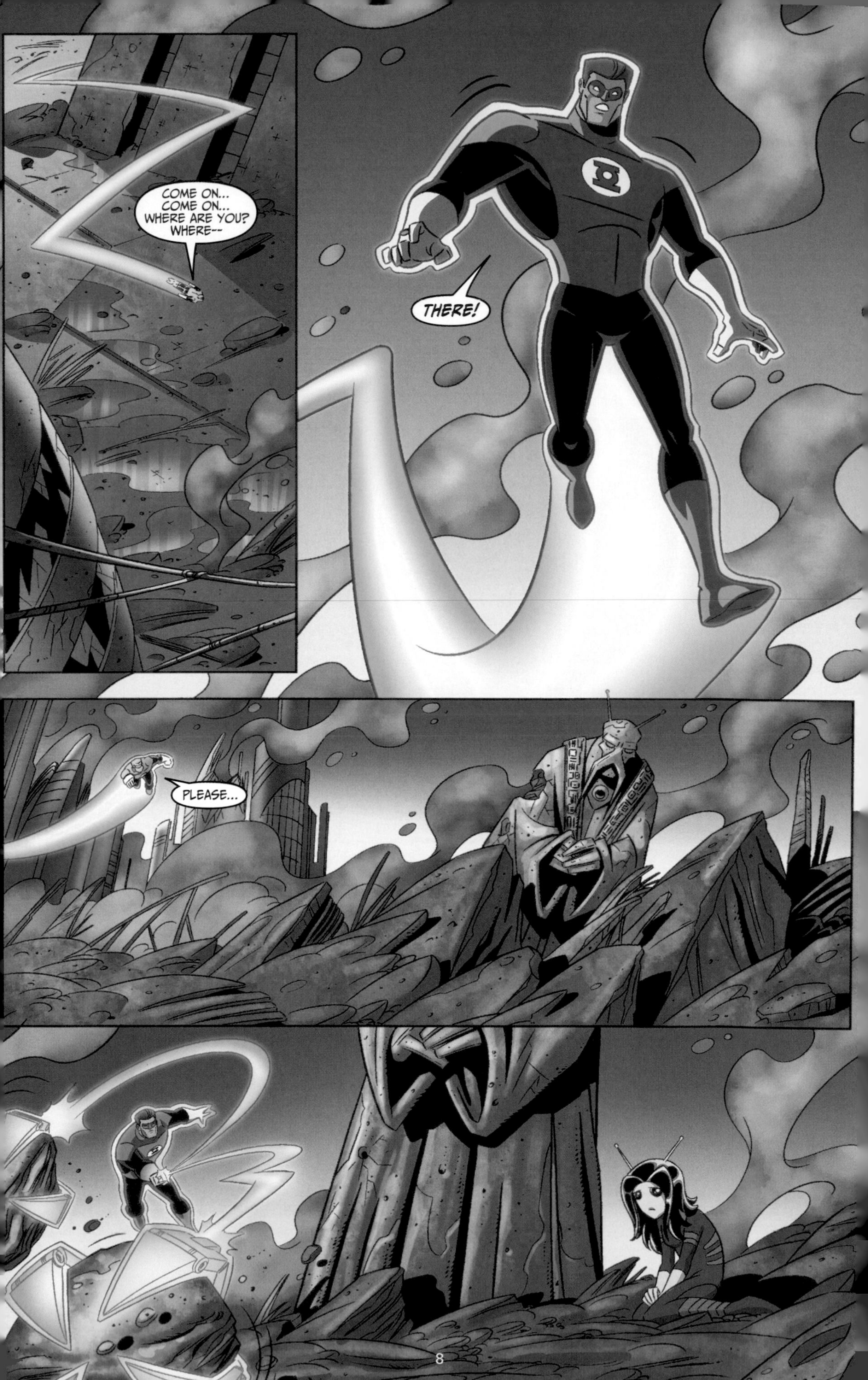
COME ON... COME ON... WHERE ARE YOU? WHERE--
THERE!
PLEASE...

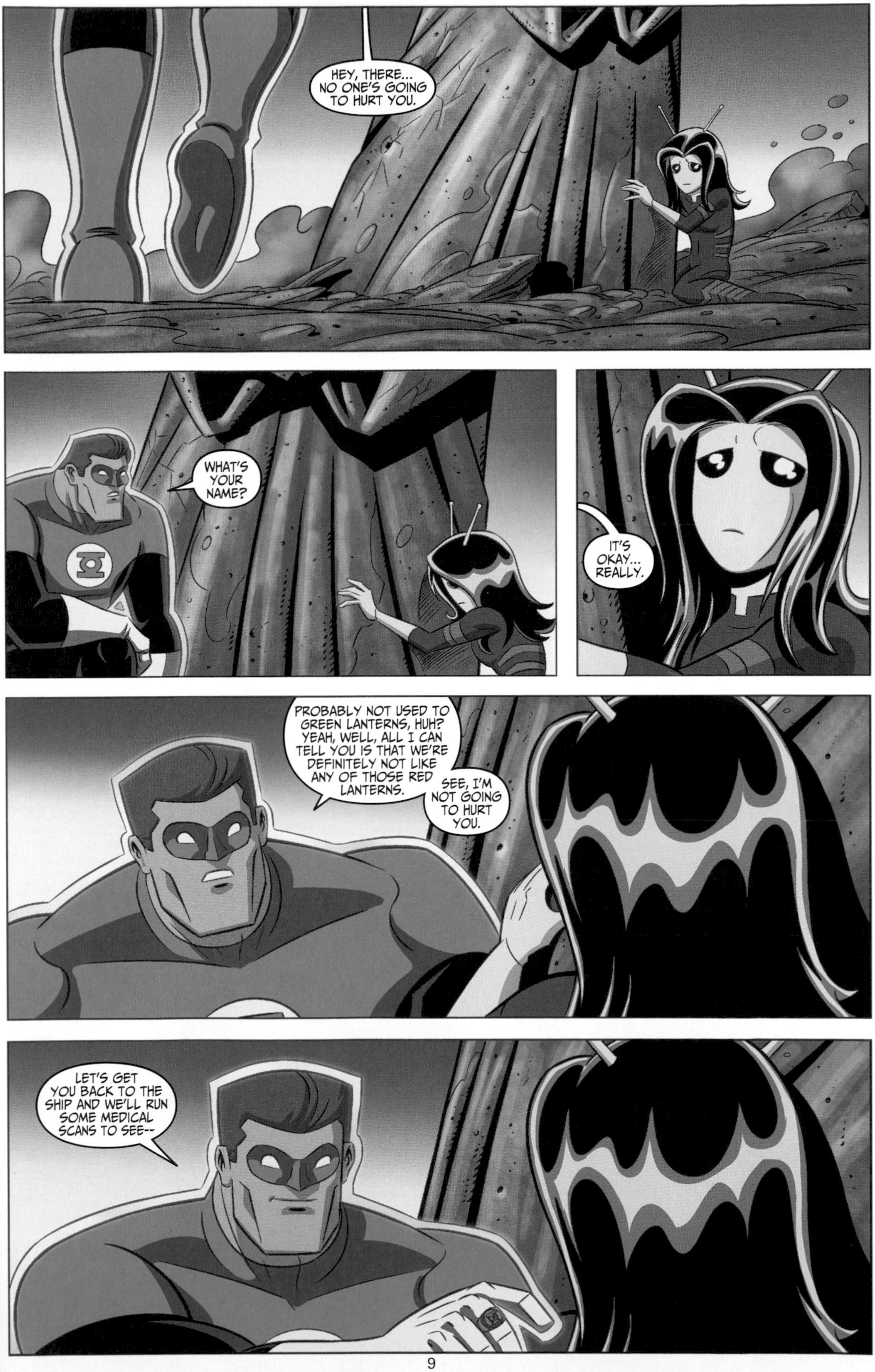
HEY, THERE... NO ONE'S GOING TO HURT YOU.
WHAT'S YOUR NAME?
IT'S OKAY... REALLY.
PROBABLY NOT USED TO GREEN LANTERNS, HUH? YEAH, WELL, ALL I CAN TELL YOU IS THAT WE'RE DEFINITELY NOT LIKE ANY OF THOSE RED LANTERNS.
SEE, I'M NOT GOING TO HURT YOU.
LET'S GET YOU BACK TO THE SHIP AND WE'LL RUN SOME MEDICAL SCANS TO SEE--

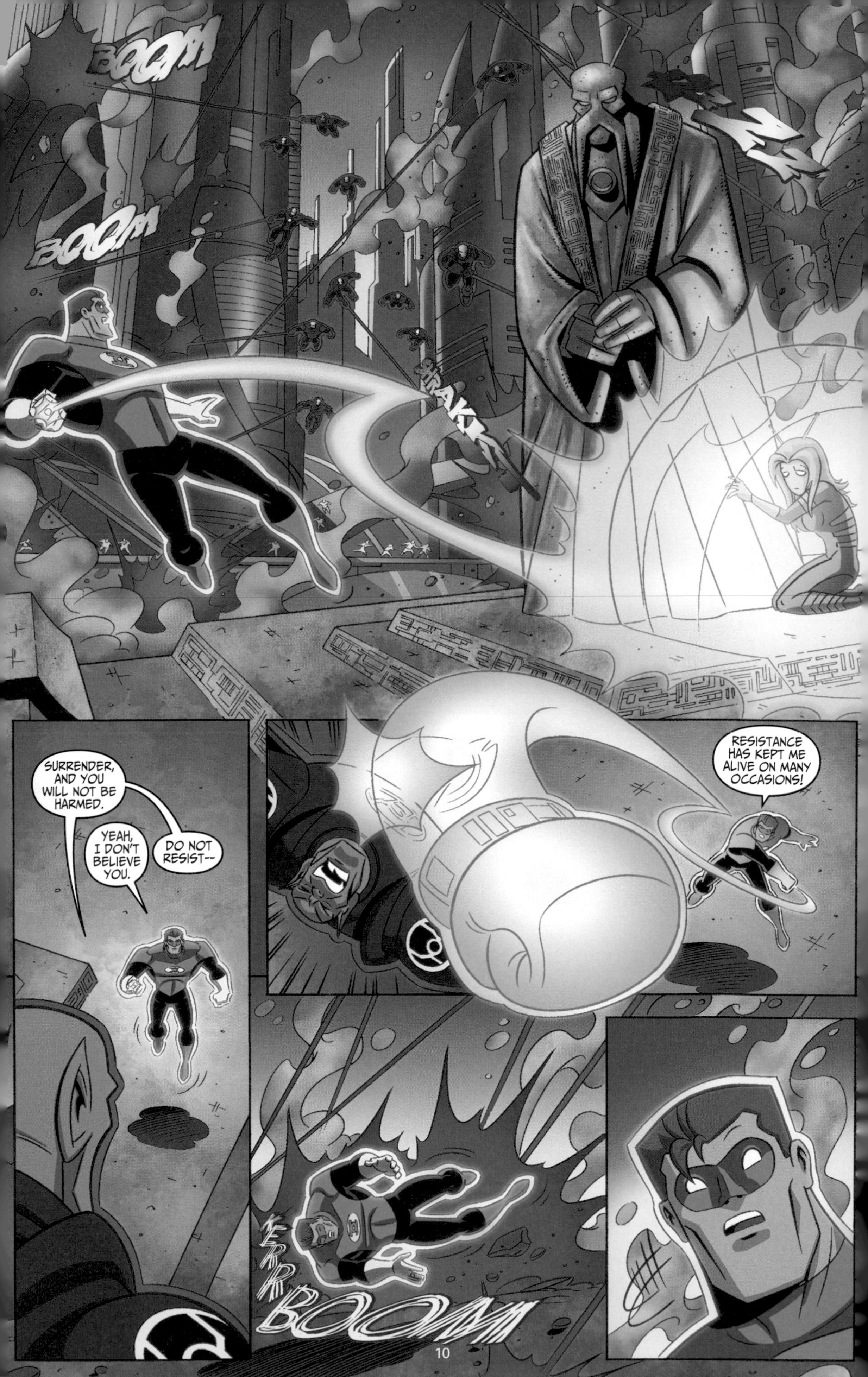
BOOM
BOOM
SHRAKK
SURRENDER, AND YOU WILL NOT BE HARMED.
YEAH, I DON'T BELIEVE YOU.
DO NOT RESIST--
RESISTANCE HAS KEPT ME ALIVE ON MANY OCCASIONS!
KERR BOOM

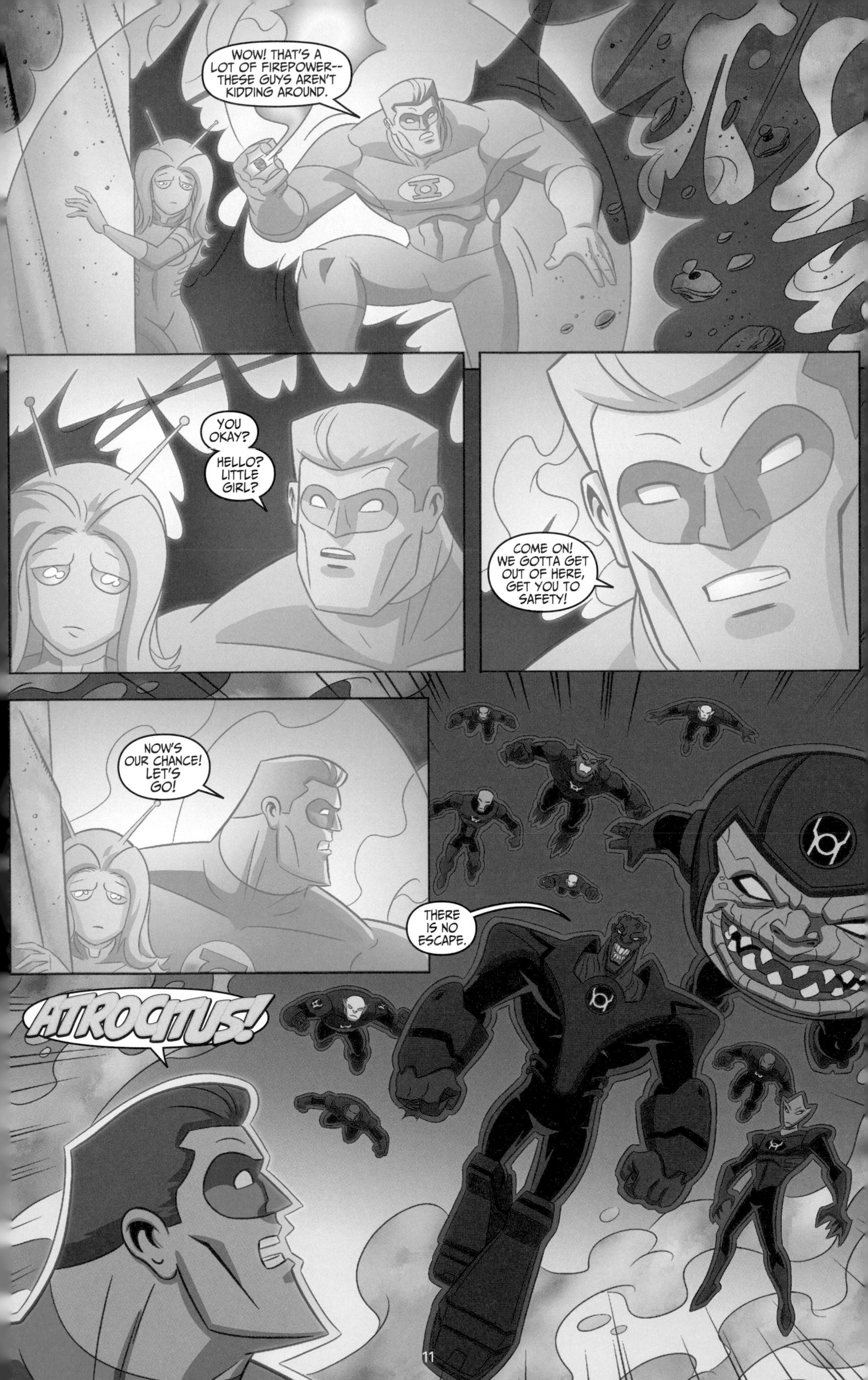
WOW! THAT'S A LOT OF FIREPOWER-- THESE GUYS AREN'T KIDDING AROUND.
YOU OKAY?
HELLO? LITTLE GIRL?
COME ON! WE GOTTA GET OUT OF HERE, GET YOU TO SAFETY!
NOW'S OUR CHANCE! LET'S GO!
THERE IS NO ESCAPE.
ATROCITUS!

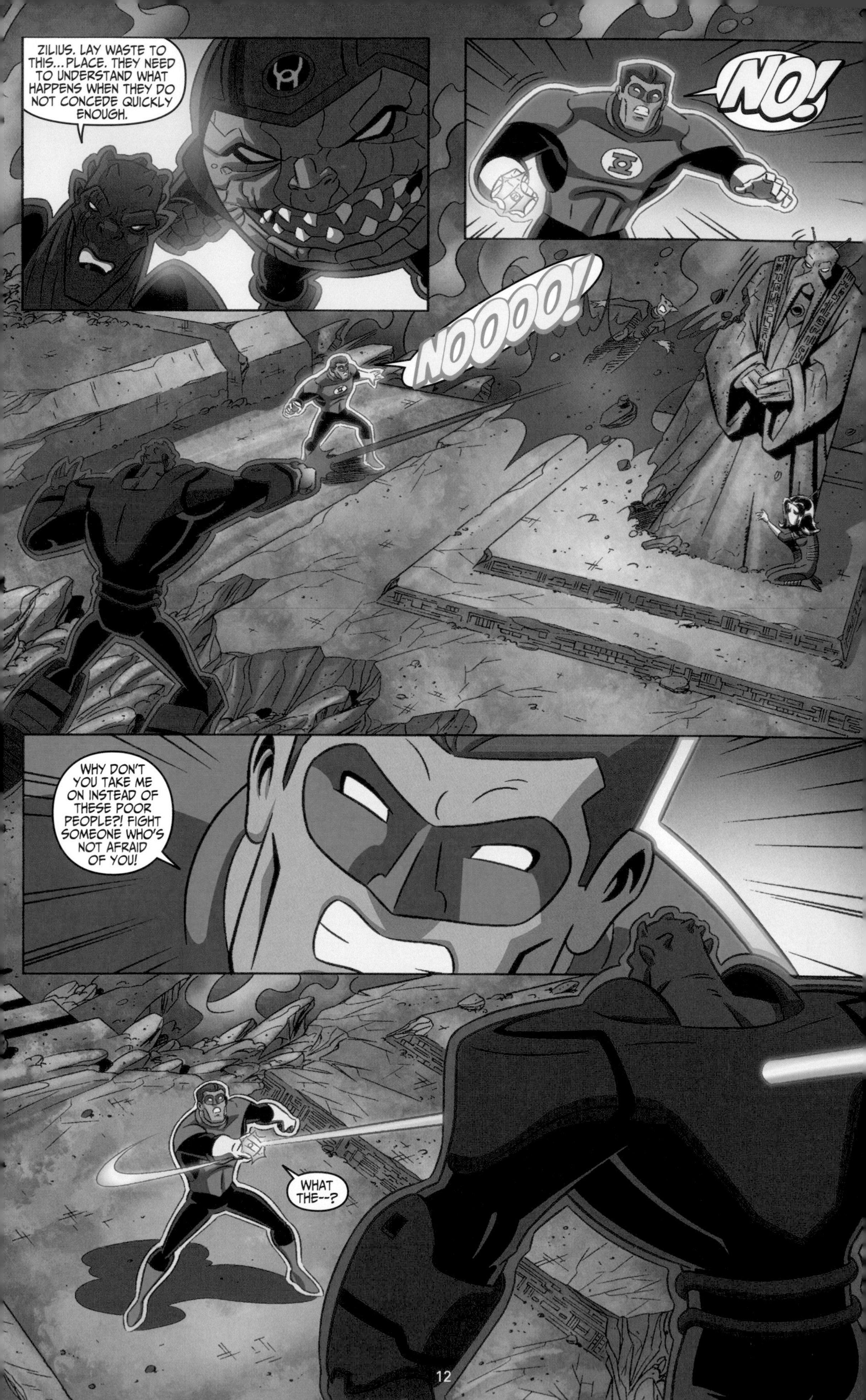
ZILIUS. LAY WASTE TO THIS...PLACE. THEY NEED TO UNDERSTAND WHAT HAPPENS WHEN THEY DO NOT CONCEDE QUICKLY ENOUGH.
NO!
NOOOOO!
WHY DON'T YOU TAKE ME ON INSTEAD OF THESE POOR PEOPLE?! FIGHT SOMEONE WHO'S NOT AFRAID OF YOU!
WHAT THE--?

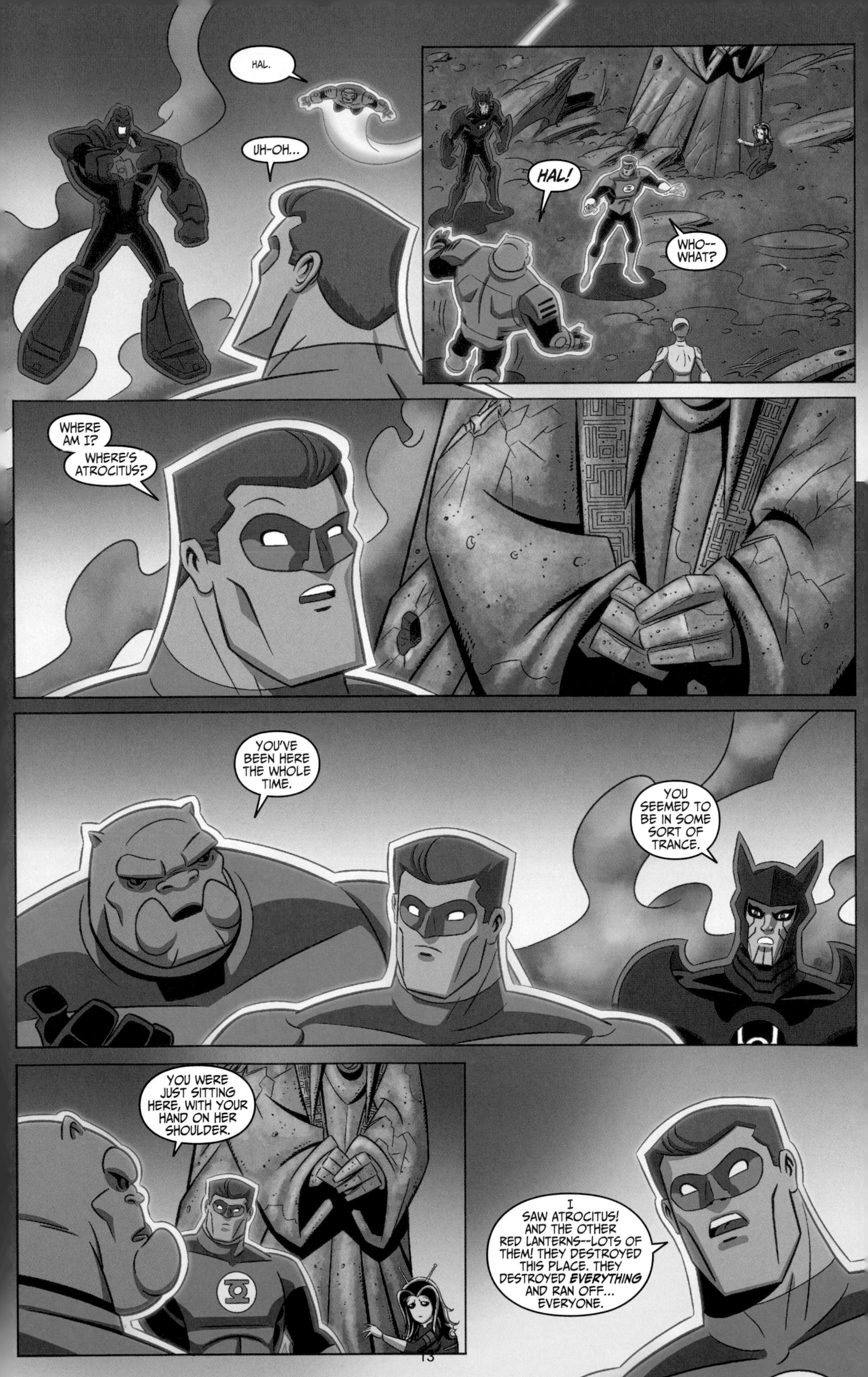
HAL.
UH-OH...
HAL!
WHO--WHAT?
WHERE AM I?
WHERE'S ATROCITUS?
YOU'VE BEEN HERE THE WHOLE TIME.
YOU SEEMED TO BE IN SOME SORT OF TRANCE.
YOU WERE JUST SITTING HERE, WITH YOUR HAND ON HER SHOULDER.
I SAW ATROCITUS! AND THE OTHER RED LANTERNS--LOTS OF THEM! THEY DESTROYED THIS PLACE. THEY DESTROYED *EVERYTHING* AND RAN OFF... EVERYONE.

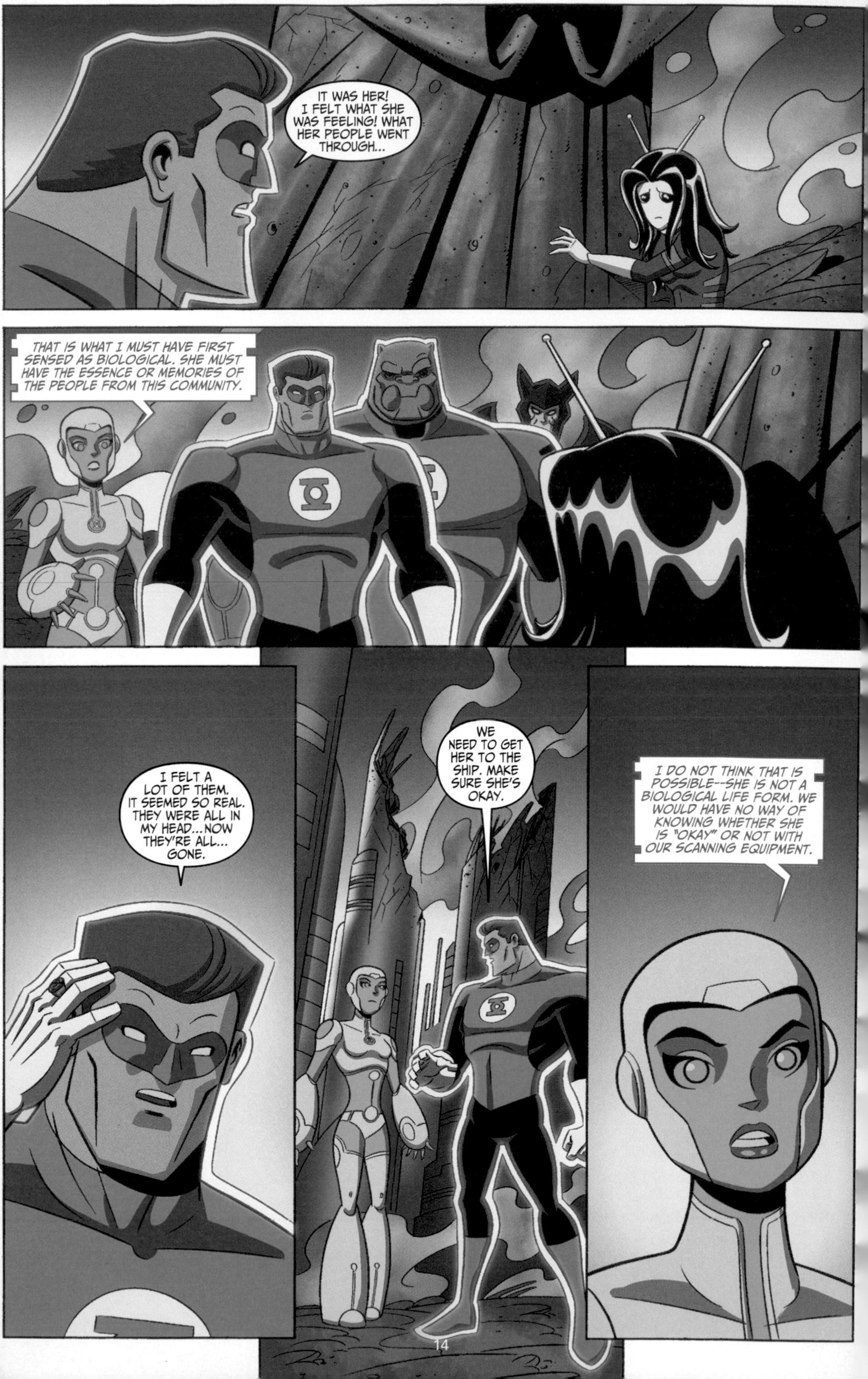
IT WAS HER! I FELT WHAT SHE WAS FEELING! WHAT HER PEOPLE WENT THROUGH...
THAT IS WHAT I MUST HAVE FIRST SENSED AS BIOLOGICAL. SHE MUST HAVE THE ESSENCE OR MEMORIES OF THE PEOPLE FROM THIS COMMUNITY.
I FELT A LOT OF THEM. IT SEEMED SO REAL. THEY WERE ALL IN MY HEAD...NOW THEY'RE ALL... GONE.
WE NEED TO GET HER TO THE SHIP. MAKE SURE SHE'S OKAY.
I DO NOT THINK THAT IS POSSIBLE--SHE IS NOT A BIOLOGICAL LIFE FORM. WE WOULD HAVE NO WAY OF KNOWING WHETHER SHE IS "OKAY" OR NOT WITH OUR SCANNING EQUIPMENT.

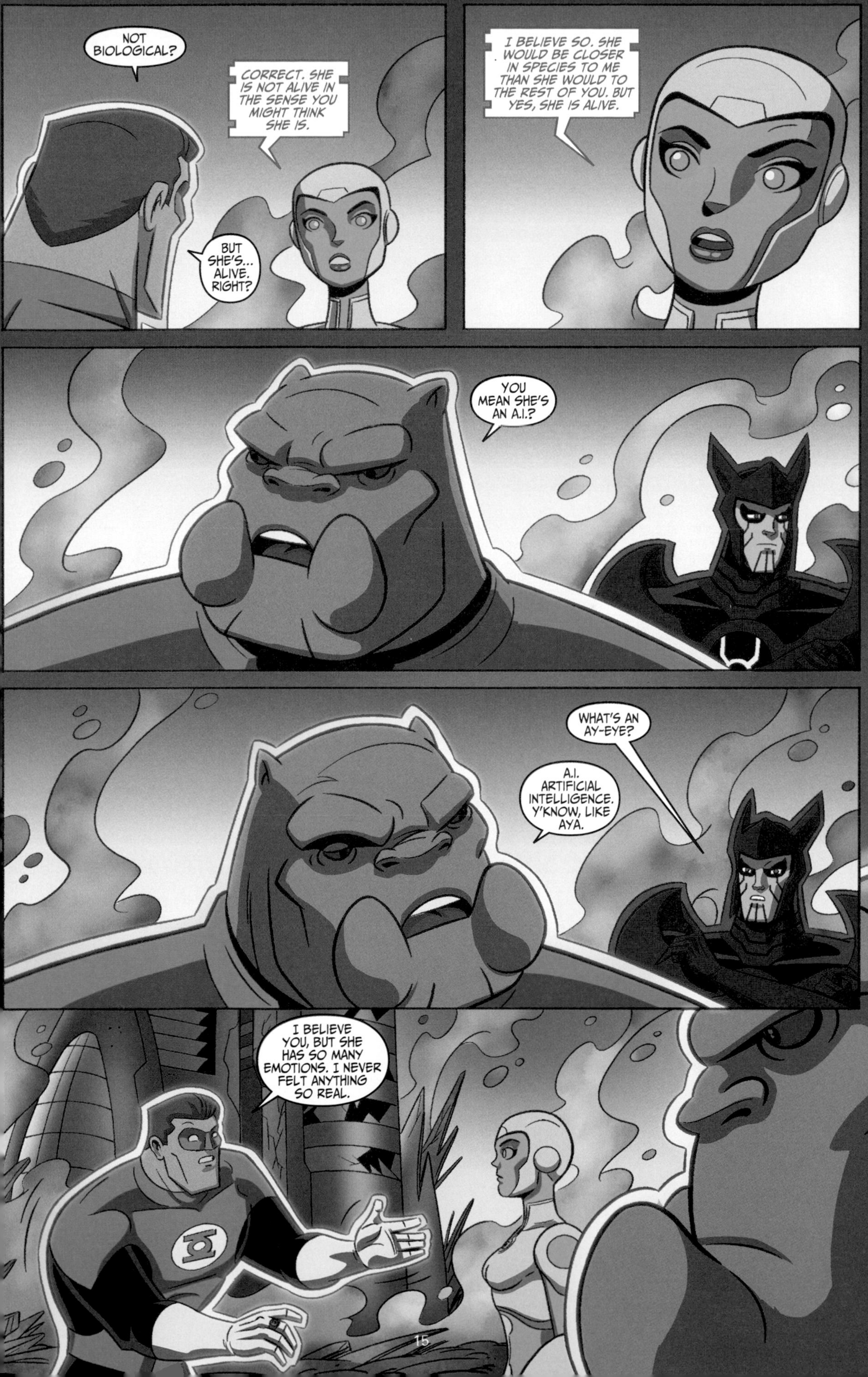
NOT BIOLOGICAL?
CORRECT. SHE IS NOT ALIVE IN THE SENSE YOU MIGHT THINK SHE IS.
BUT SHE'S... ALIVE. RIGHT?
I BELIEVE SO. SHE WOULD BE CLOSER IN SPECIES TO ME THAN SHE WOULD TO THE REST OF YOU. BUT YES, SHE IS ALIVE.
YOU MEAN SHE'S AN A.I.?
WHAT'S AN AY-EYE?
A.I. ARTIFICIAL INTELLIGENCE. Y'KNOW, LIKE AYA.
I BELIEVE YOU, BUT SHE HAS SO MANY EMOTIONS. I NEVER FELT ANYTHING SO REAL.

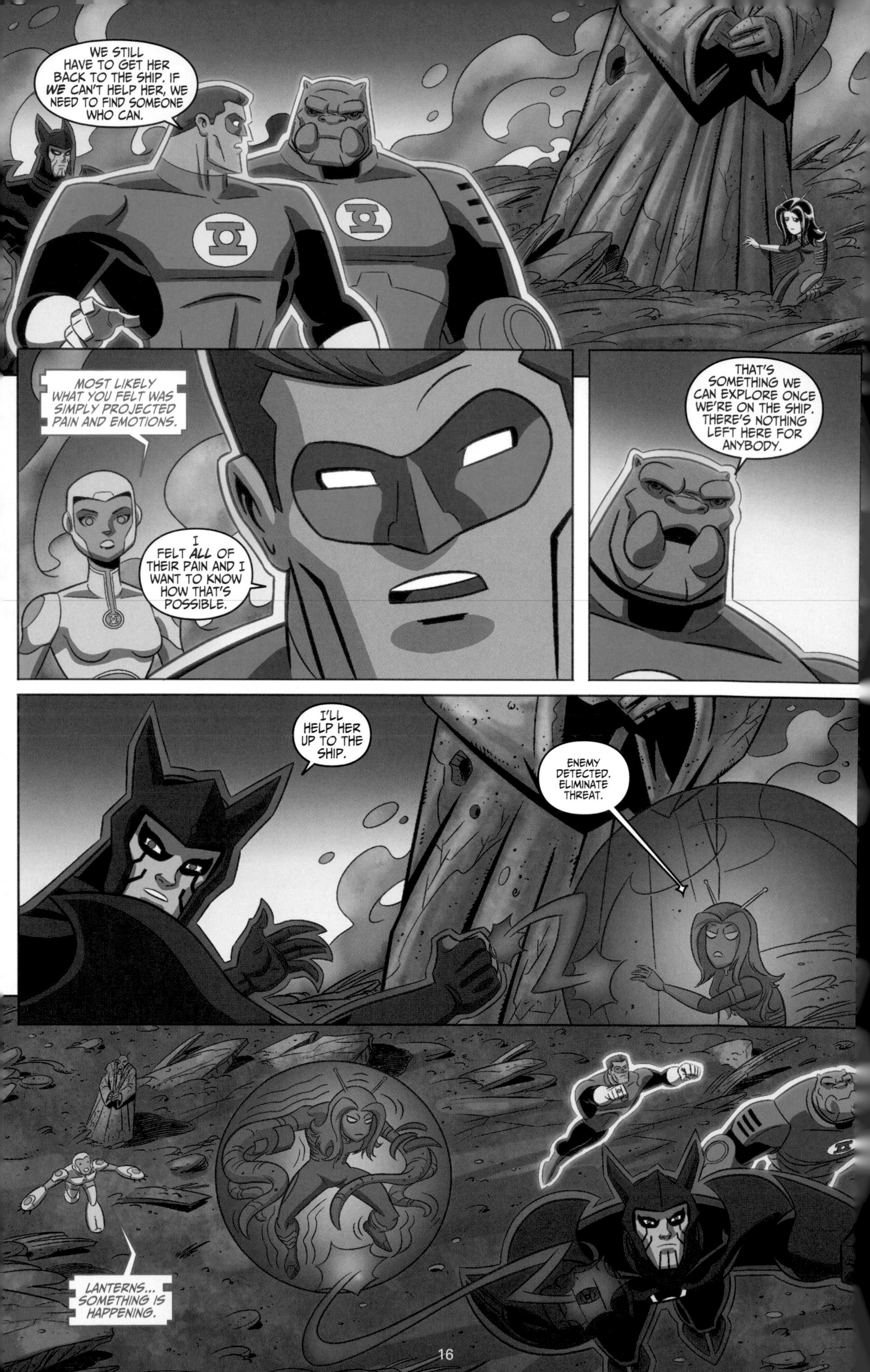
WE STILL HAVE TO GET HER BACK TO THE SHIP. IF WE CAN'T HELP HER, WE NEED TO FIND SOMEONE WHO CAN.
MOST LIKELY WHAT YOU FELT WAS SIMPLY PROJECTED PAIN AND EMOTIONS.
I FELT ALL OF THEIR PAIN AND I WANT TO KNOW HOW THAT'S POSSIBLE.
THAT'S SOMETHING WE CAN EXPLORE ONCE WE'RE ON THE SHIP. THERE'S NOTHING LEFT HERE FOR ANYBODY.
I'LL HELP HER UP TO THE SHIP.
ENEMY DETECTED. ELIMINATE THREAT.
LANTERNS... SOMETHING IS HAPPENING.

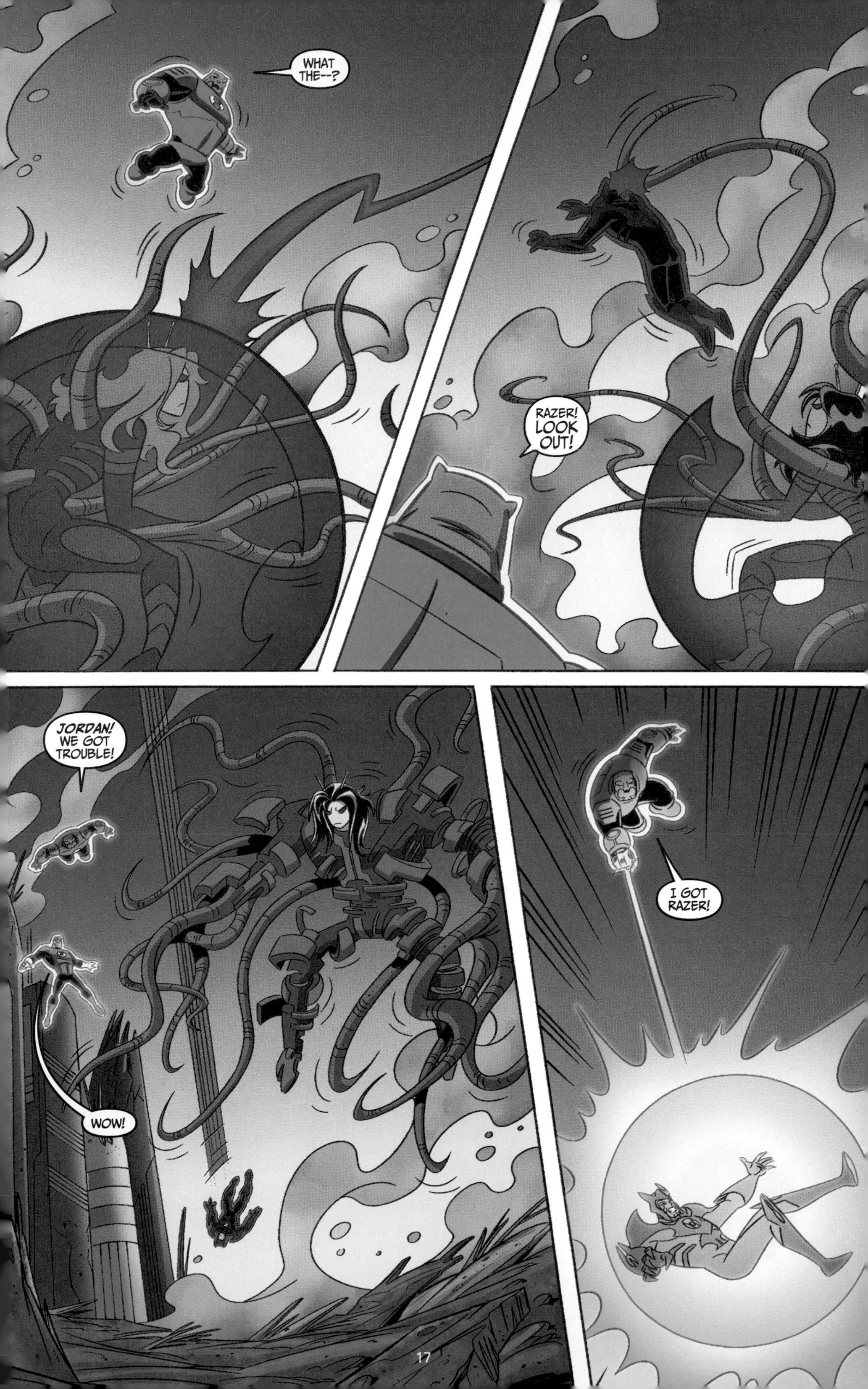
WHAT THE--?
RAZER! LOOK OUT!
JORDAN! WE GOT TROUBLE!
WOW!
I GOT RAZER!

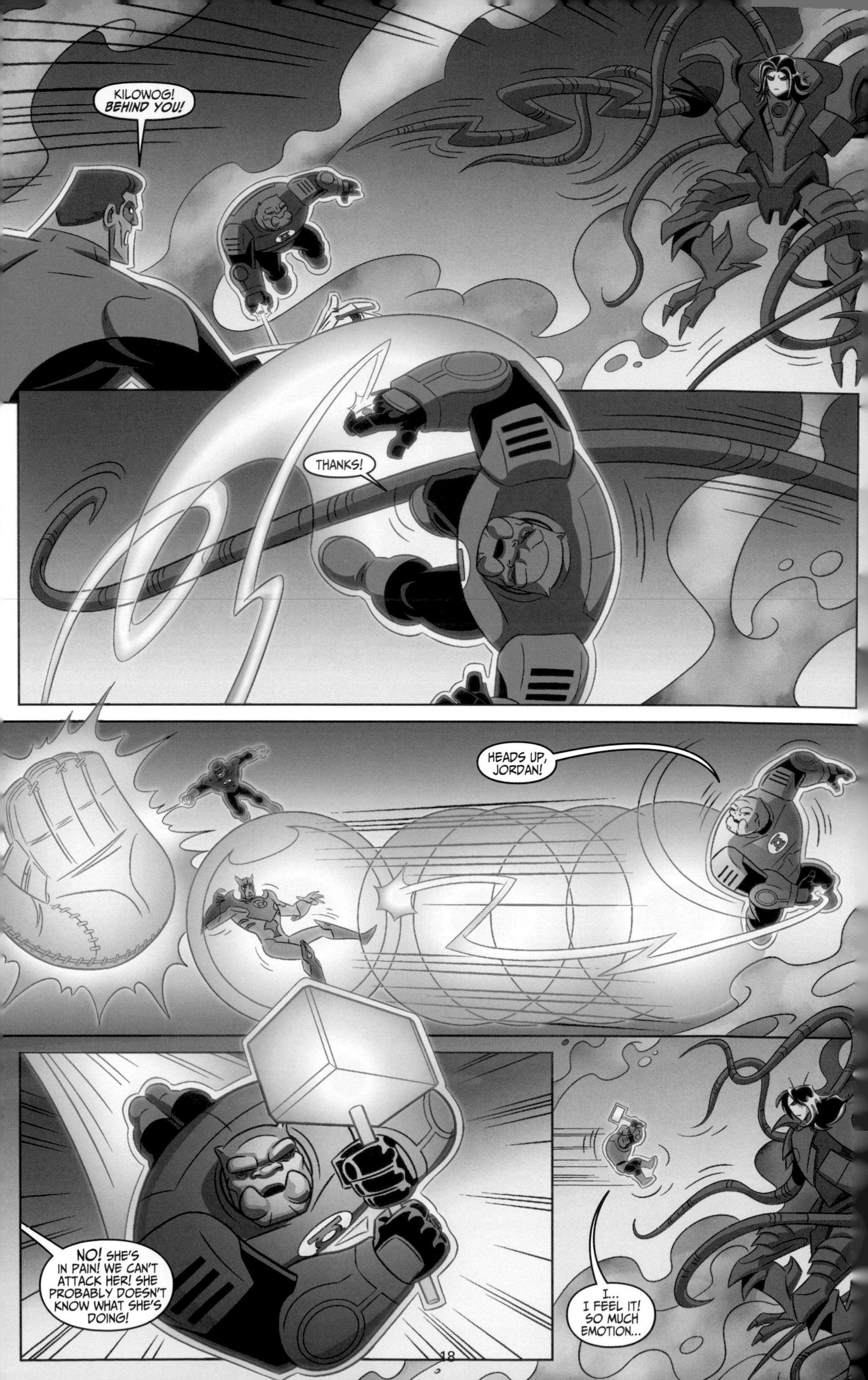
KILOWOG! BEHIND YOU!
THANKS!
HEADS UP, JORDAN!
NO! SHE'S IN PAIN! WE CAN'T ATTACK HER! SHE PROBABLY DOESN'T KNOW WHAT SHE'S DOING!
I... I FEEL IT! SO MUCH EMOTION...

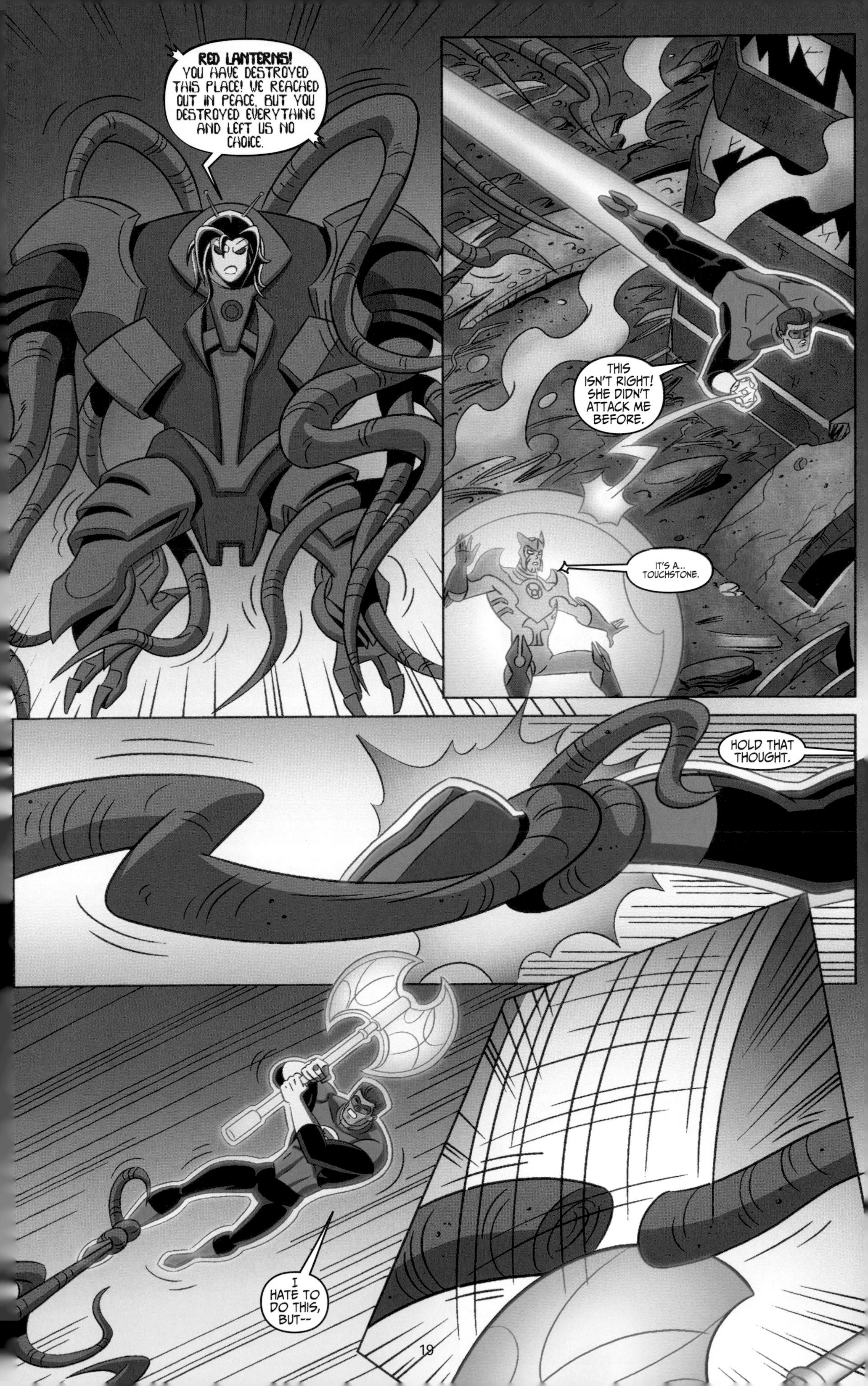
RED LANTERNS! YOU HAVE DESTROYED THIS PLACE! WE REACHED OUT IN PEACE, BUT YOU DESTROYED EVERYTHING AND LEFT US NO CHOICE.
THIS ISN'T RIGHT! SHE DIDN'T ATTACK ME BEFORE.
IT'S A... TOUCHSTONE.
HOLD THAT THOUGHT.
I HATE TO DO THIS, BUT--

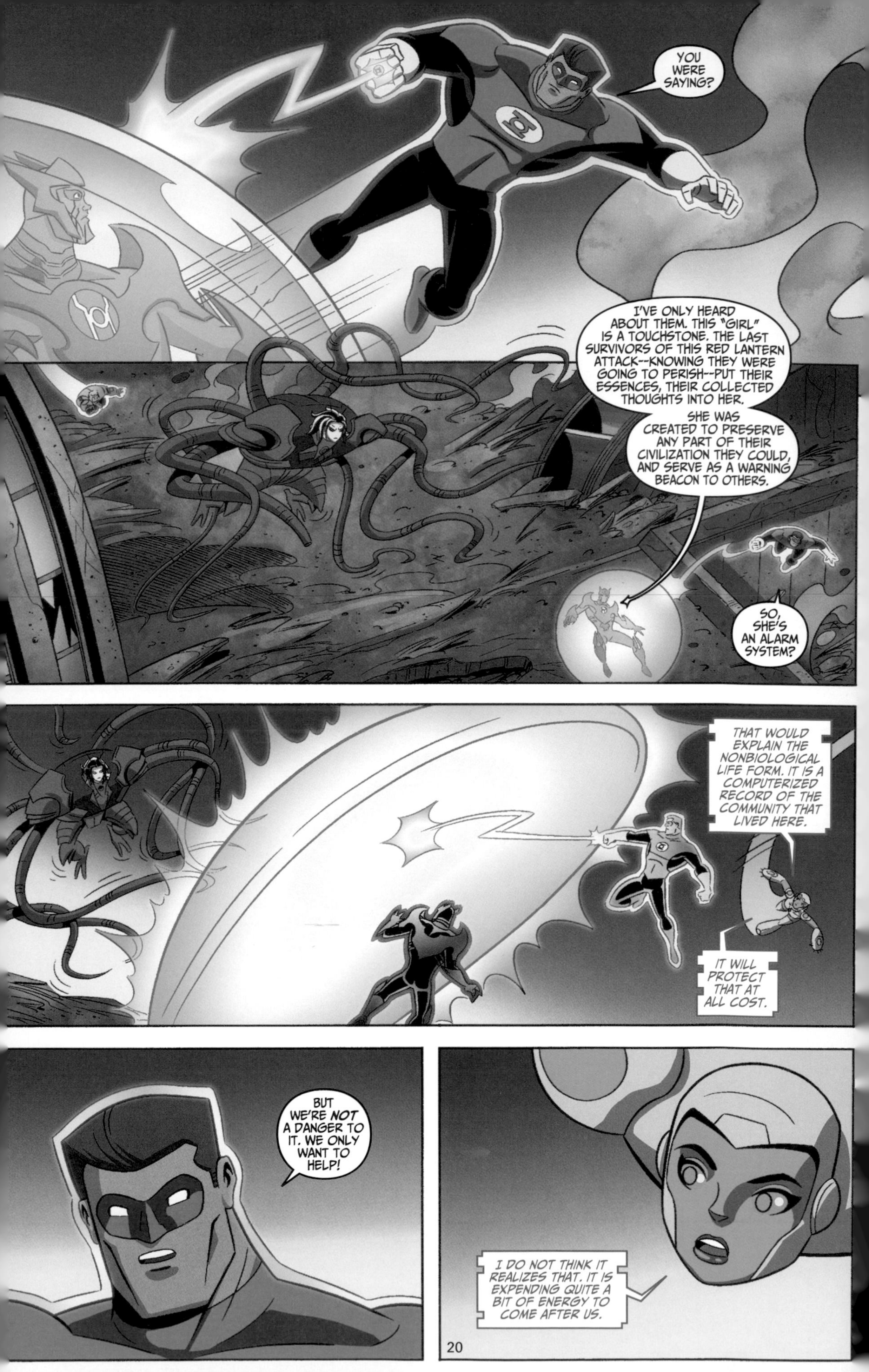
YOU WERE SAYING?
I'VE ONLY HEARD ABOUT THEM. THIS "GIRL" IS A TOUCHSTONE. THE LAST SURVIVORS OF THIS RED LANTERN ATTACK--KNOWING THEY WERE GOING TO PERISH--PUT THEIR ESSENCES, THEIR COLLECTED THOUGHTS INTO HER.
SHE WAS CREATED TO PRESERVE ANY PART OF THEIR CIVILIZATION THEY COULD, AND SERVE AS A WARNING BEACON TO OTHERS.
SO, SHE'S AN ALARM SYSTEM?
THAT WOULD EXPLAIN THE NONBIOLOGICAL LIFE FORM. IT IS A COMPUTERIZED RECORD OF THE COMMUNITY THAT LIVED HERE.
IT WILL PROTECT THAT AT ALL COST.
BUT WE'RE NOT A DANGER TO IT. WE ONLY WANT TO HELP!
I DO NOT THINK IT REALIZES THAT. IT IS EXPENDING QUITE A BIT OF ENERGY TO COME AFTER US.

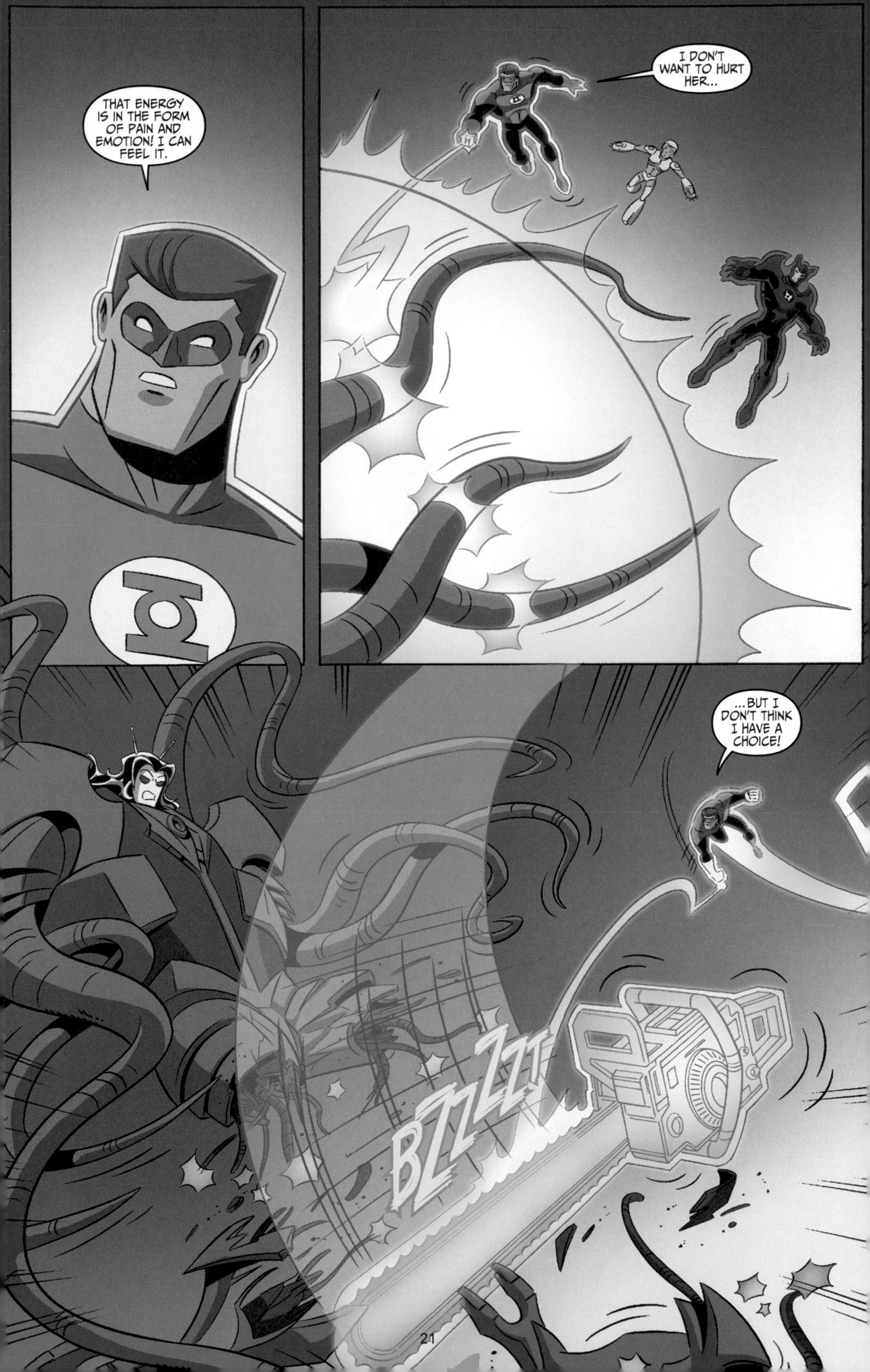
THAT ENERGY IS IN THE FORM OF PAIN AND EMOTION! I CAN FEEL IT.
I DON'T WANT TO HURT HER...
...BUT I DON'T THINK I HAVE A CHOICE!
BZZZZZT

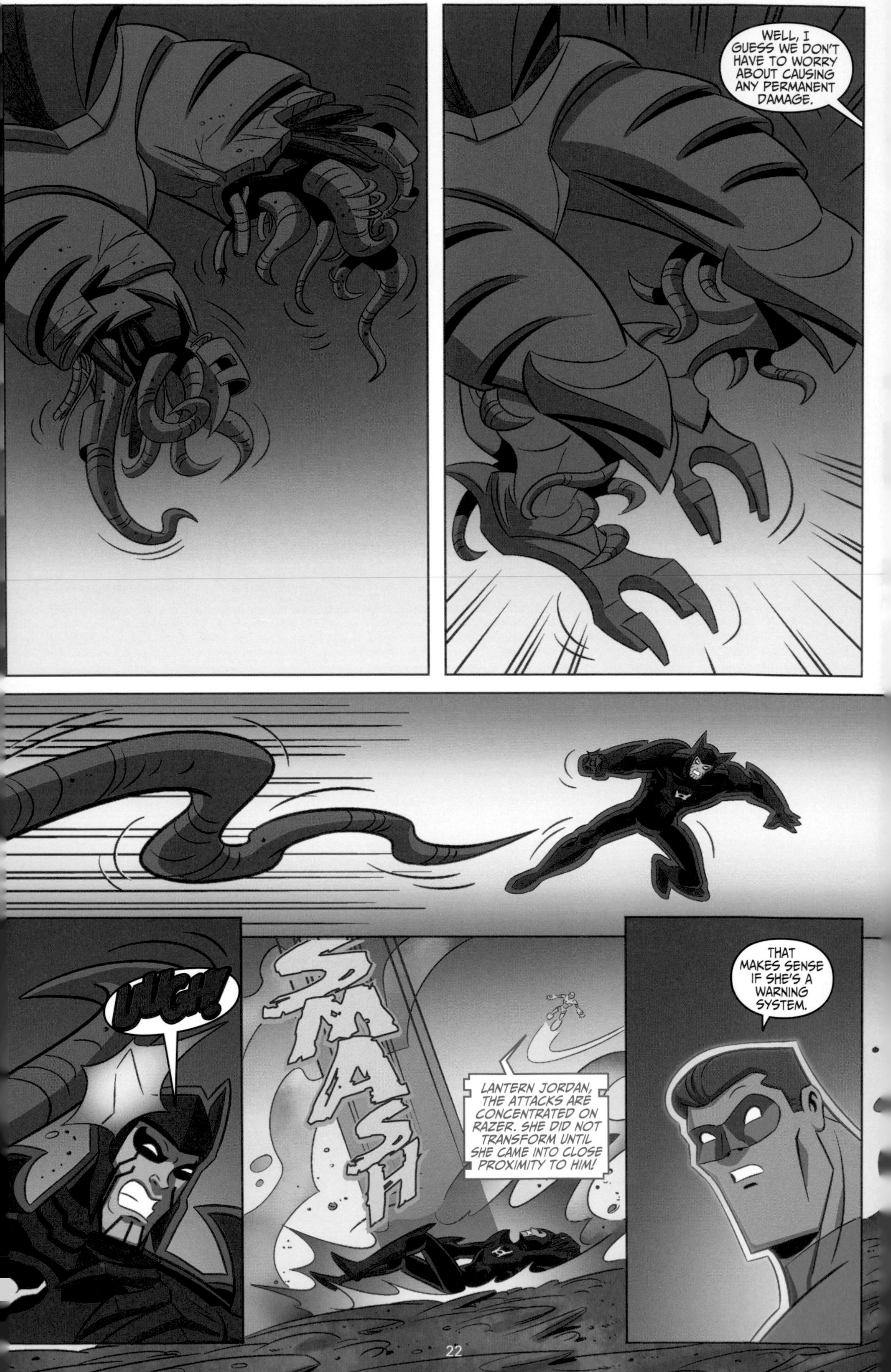
WELL, I GUESS WE DON'T HAVE TO WORRY ABOUT CAUSING ANY PERMANENT DAMAGE.
UGH!
SMASH
LANTERN JORDAN, THE ATTACKS ARE CONCENTRATED ON RAZER. SHE DID NOT TRANSFORM UNTIL SHE CAME INTO CLOSE PROXIMITY TO HIM!
THAT MAKES SENSE IF SHE'S A WARNING SYSTEM.

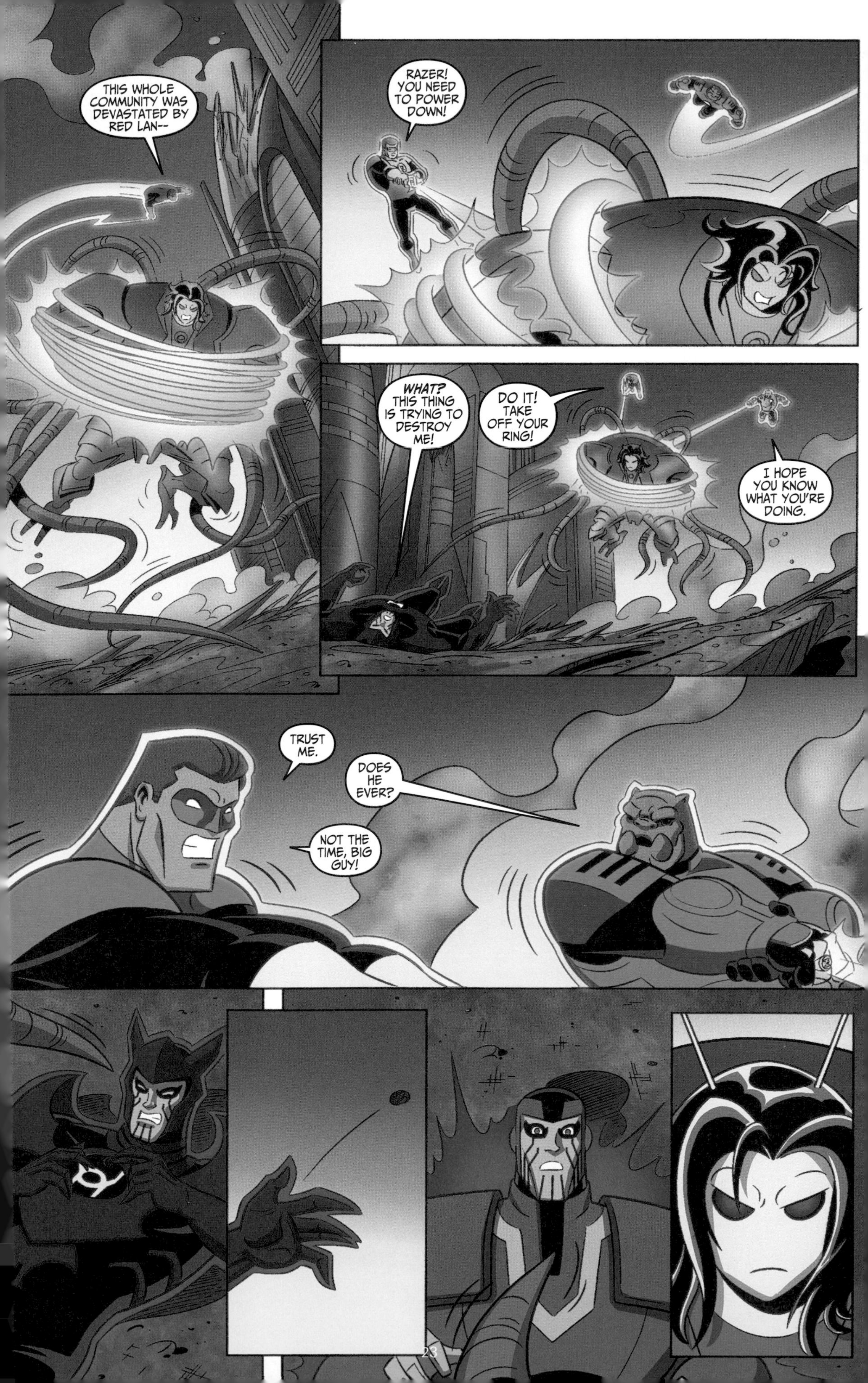
THIS WHOLE COMMUNITY WAS DEVASTATED BY RED LAN--
RAZER! YOU NEED TO POWER DOWN!
WHAT? THIS THING IS TRYING TO DESTROY ME!
DO IT! TAKE OFF YOUR RING!
I HOPE YOU KNOW WHAT YOU'RE DOING.
TRUST ME.
DOES HE EVER?
NOT THE TIME, BIG GUY!

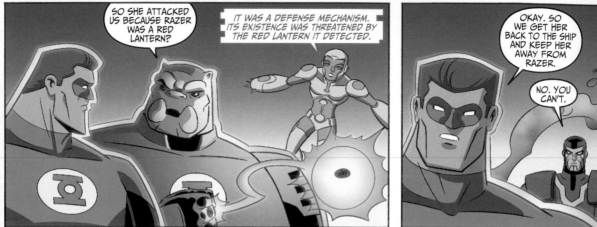

SO SHE ATTACKED US BECAUSE RAZER WAS A RED LANTERN?

IT WAS A DEFENSE MECHANISM. ITS EXISTENCE WAS THREATENED BY THE RED LANTERN IT DETECTED.

OKAY. SO WE GET HER BACK TO THE SHIP AND KEEP HER AWAY FROM RAZER.

NO. YOU CAN'T.

FROM WHAT I KNOW OF TOUCHSTONES, YOU CAN'T DO THAT. IF YOU REMOVE HER, THIS LITTLE GIRL WILL MORPH INTO THAT THING WE WERE FIGHTING. IT WILL DO ANYTHING TO GET BACK TO THIS SPOT.

SO WE HAVE TO LEAVE HER HERE? THAT'S CRUEL!

NO. IT'S NOT CRUEL. THIS IS WHY SHE WAS CREATED. THIS IS HER PURPOSE, TO TELL THE STORY OF HER PEOPLE FOR ANY TRAVELERS PASSING THIS WAY.

WE HAVE NO CHOICE BUT TO LEAVE HER HERE.

...GOODBYE, GREEN LANTERN.

END

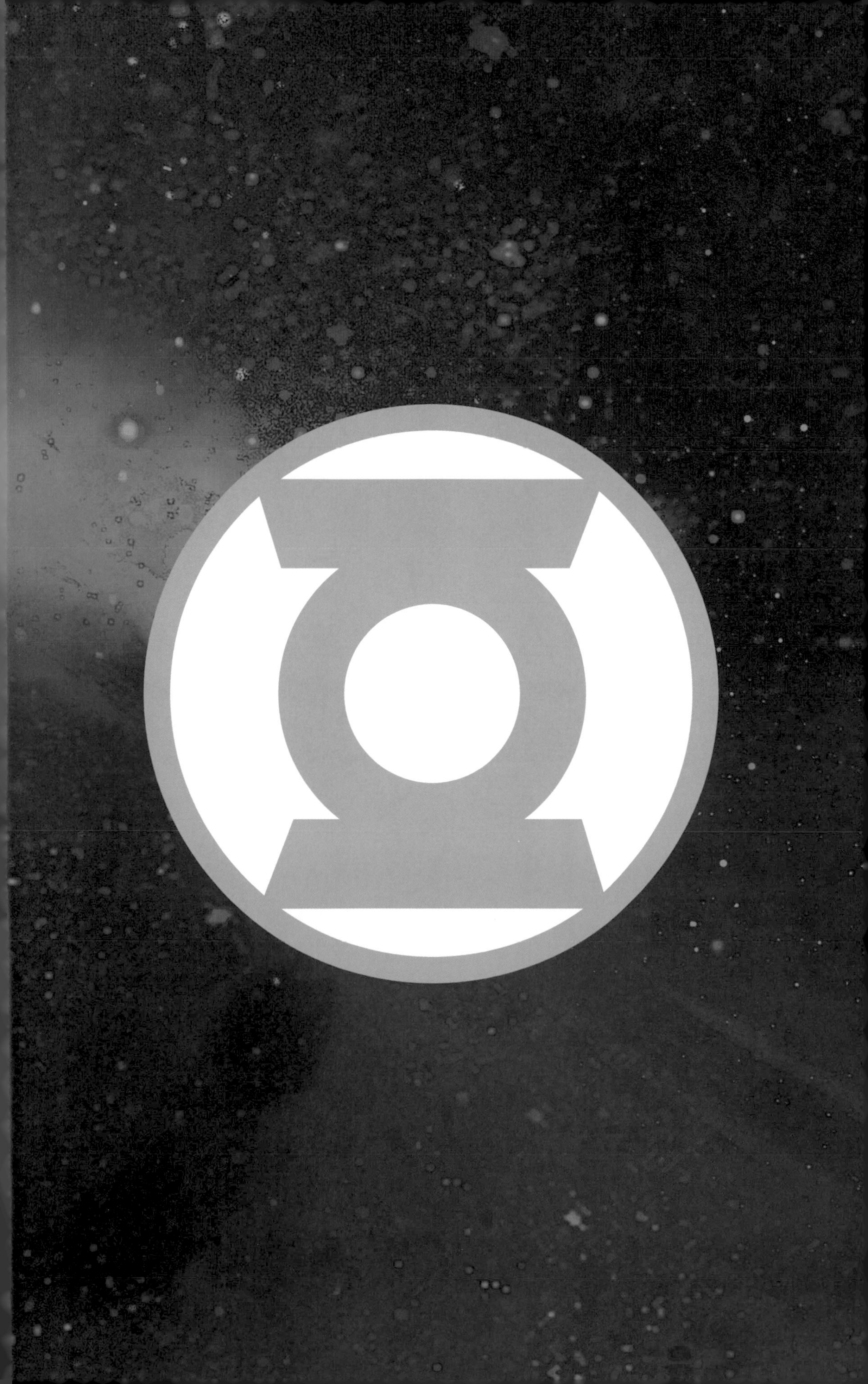

DRAW YOUR OWN GREEN LANTERN AYA!

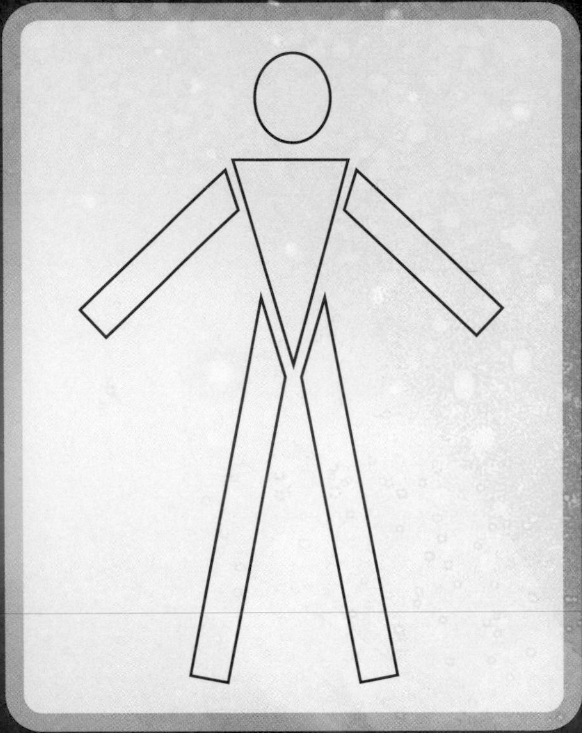

1.) Using a pencil, start with some basic shapes to build a "body."

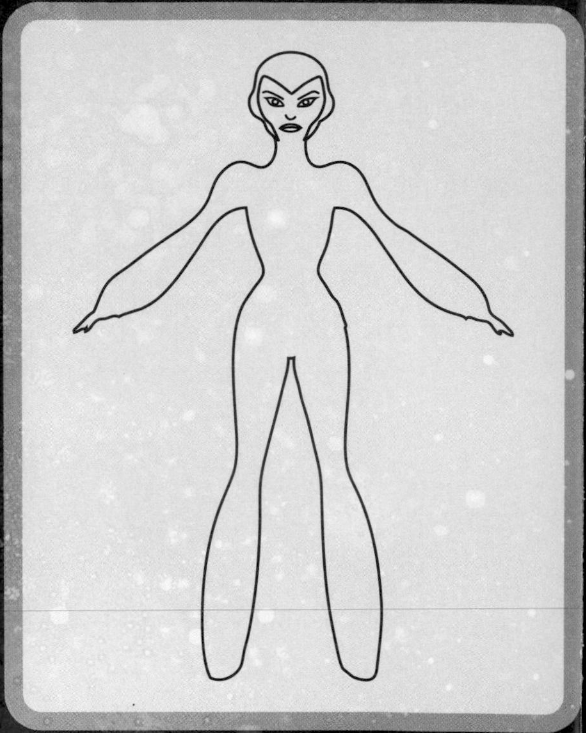

2.) Smooth your outline, and begin adding facial features.

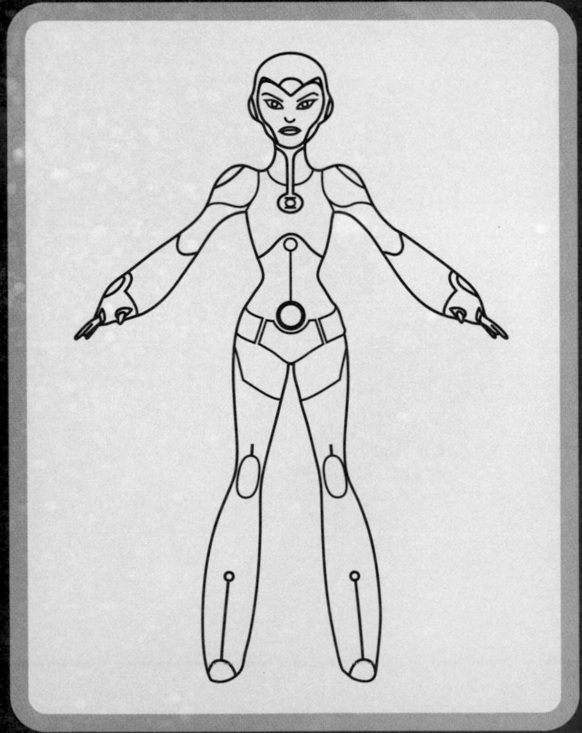

3.) Add in costume details, like Aya's suit, helmet, and Green Lantern symbol.

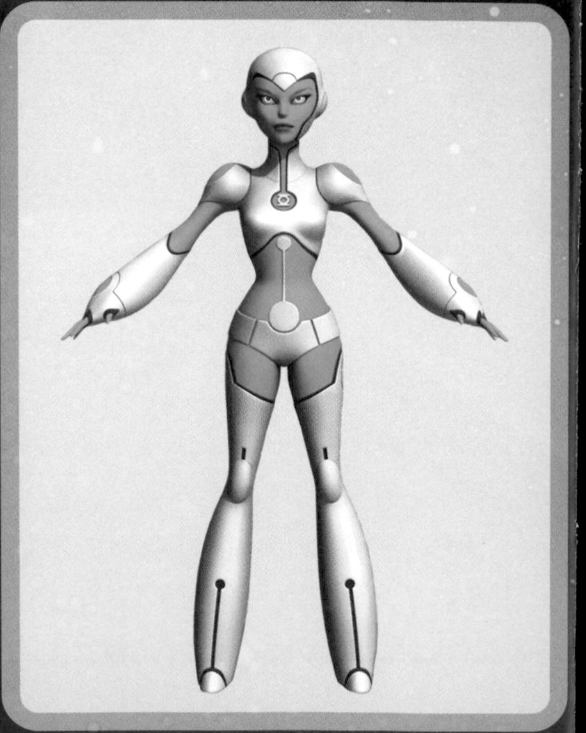

4.) Fill in the colors with crayons or markers.

CREATORS

ART BALTAZAR writer

Art Baltazar is a cartoonist machine from the heart of Chicago! He defines cartoons and comics not only as an art style, but as a way of life. Currently, Art is the creative force behind *The New York Times* best-selling, Eisner Award-winning, DC Comics series Tiny Titans, and the co-writer for *Billy Batson and the Magic of SHAZAM!* and co-creator of the Superman Family Adventures series. Art is living the dream! He draws comics and never has to leave the house. He lives with his lovely wife, Rose, big boy Sonny, little boy Gordon, and little girl Audrey. Right on!

FRANCO AURELIANI writer

Bronx, New York-born writer and artist Franco Aureliani has been drawing comics since he could hold a crayon. Currently residing in upstate New York with his wife, Ivette, and son, Nicolas, Franco spends most of his days in a Batcave-like studio where he produces DC's Tiny Titans comics. In 1995, Franco founded Blindwolf Studios, an independent art studio where he and fellow creators can create children's comics. Franco is the creator, artist, and writer of *Weirdsville*, *L'il Creeps*, and *Eagle All Star*, as well as the co-creator and writer of *Patrick the Wolf Boy*. When he's not writing and drawing, Franco also teaches high school art.

DARIO BRIZUELA illustrator

Dario Brizuela is a professional comic book artist. He's illustrated some of today's most popular characters, including Batman, Green Lantern, Teenage Mutant Ninja Turtles, Thor, Iron Man, and Transformers. His best-known works for DC Comics include the series DC Super Friends, Justice League Unlimited, and Batman: The Brave and the Bold.

GLOSSARY

concede (kuhn-SEED) — to admit something unwillingly

recurring (ri-KUR-ing) — repeating, or something that happens more than once

resistance (ri-ZISS-tuhnss) — fighting back, or a force that opposes the motion of an object

surrender (suh-REN-dur) — to give up, or to admit that you are beaten

thriving (THRYE-ving) — prospering, flourishing, or doing very well

threat (THRET) — a sign or possibility that something is harmful

trance (TRANSS) — if you are in a trance, you are in a conscious state but not really aware of what is happening around you

VISUAL QUESTIONS

1. Why did the touchstone consider Razer to be a threat? Explain your answer using examples from the story.

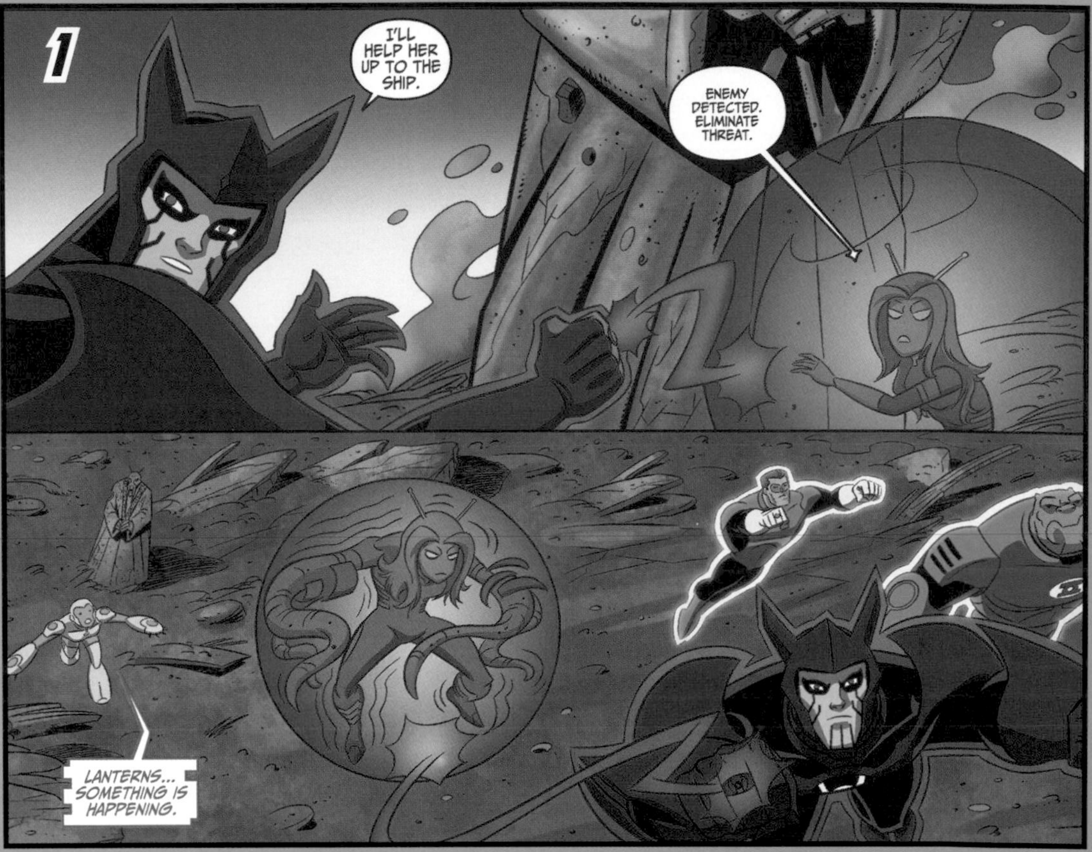
1
I'LL HELP HER UP TO THE SHIP.
ENEMY DETECTED. ELIMINATE THREAT.
LANTERNS... SOMETHING IS HAPPENING.

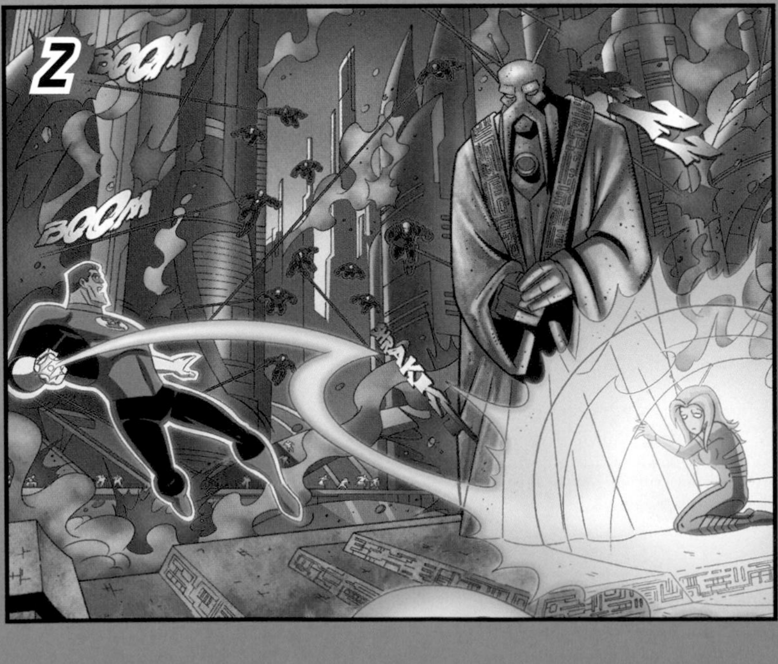
2
BOOM
BOOM
KRAKK

2. Why was the city suddenly restored before Hal's eyes when he came into contact with the touchstone character?

3. Why does the touchstone's speech bubble in the panel below look different from the other characters' speech bubbles?

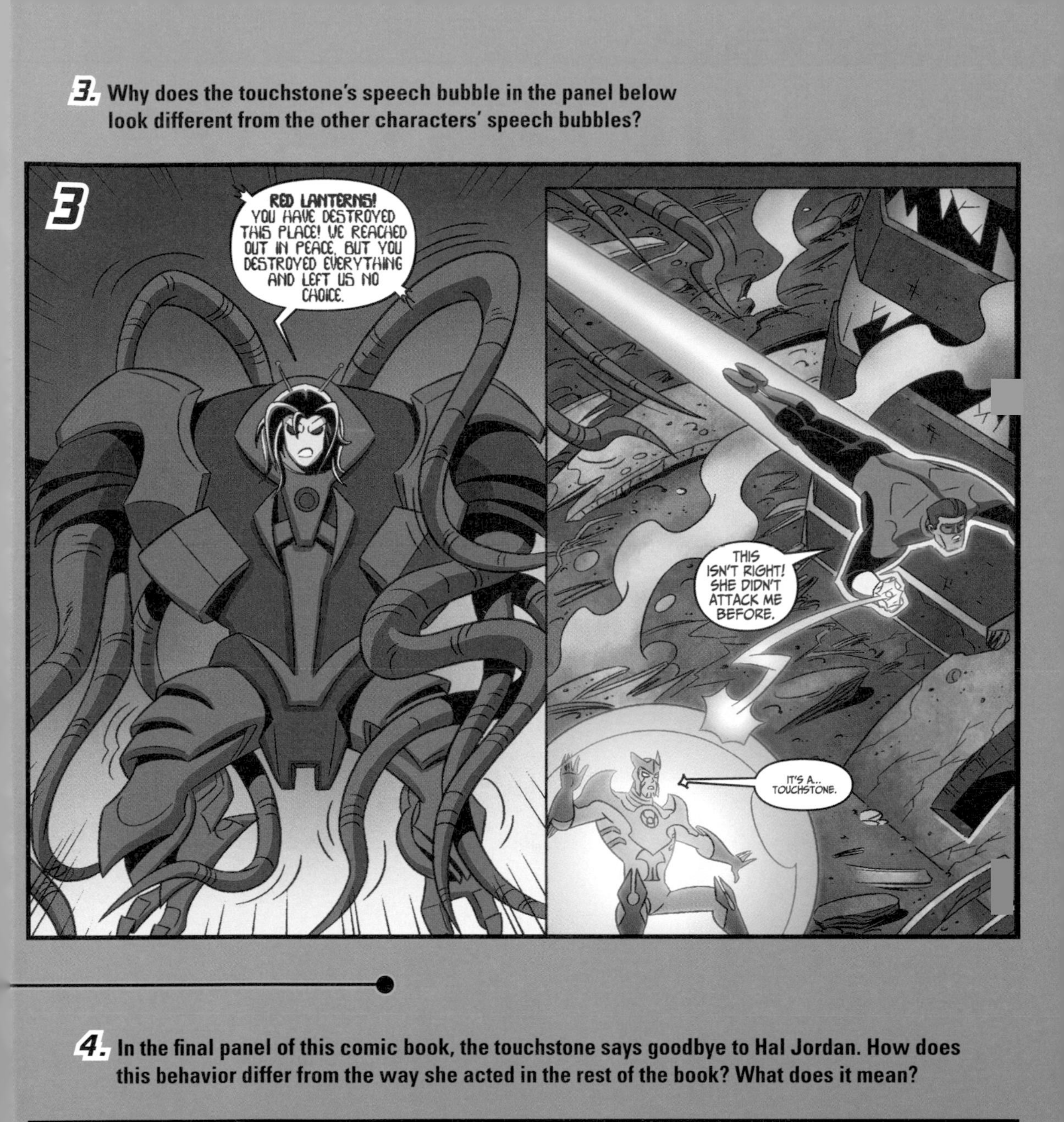

3
RED LANTERNS! YOU HAVE DESTROYED THIS PLACE! WE REACHED OUT IN PEACE, BUT YOU DESTROYED EVERYTHING AND LEFT US NO CHOICE.
THIS ISN'T RIGHT! SHE DIDN'T ATTACK ME BEFORE.
IT'S A... TOUCHSTONE.

4. In the final panel of this comic book, the touchstone says goodbye to Hal Jordan. How does this behavior differ from the way she acted in the rest of the book? What does it mean?

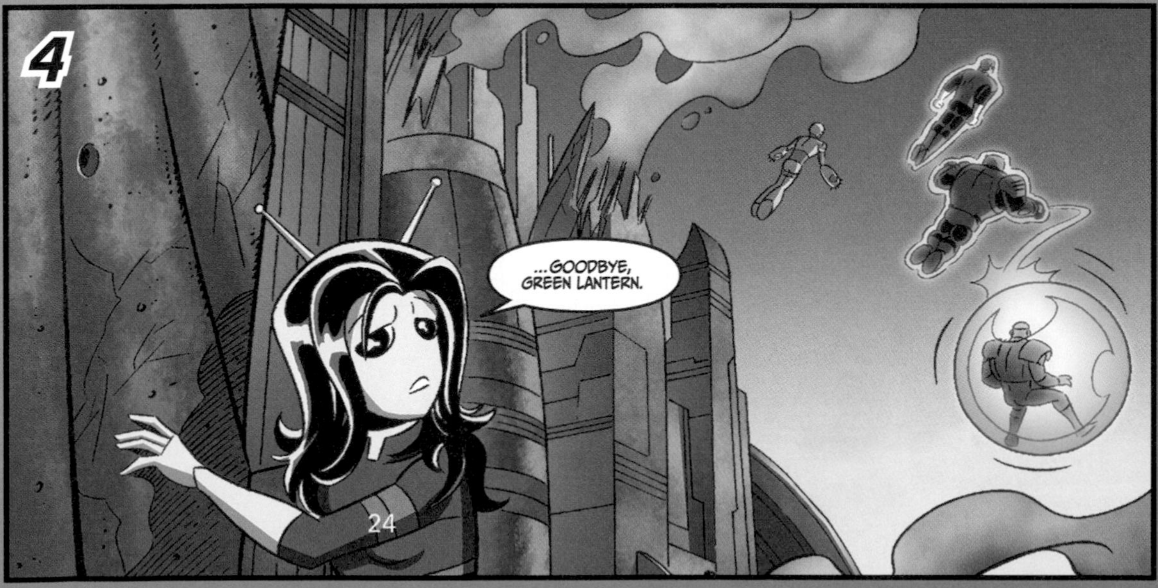

4
...GOODBYE, GREEN LANTERN.

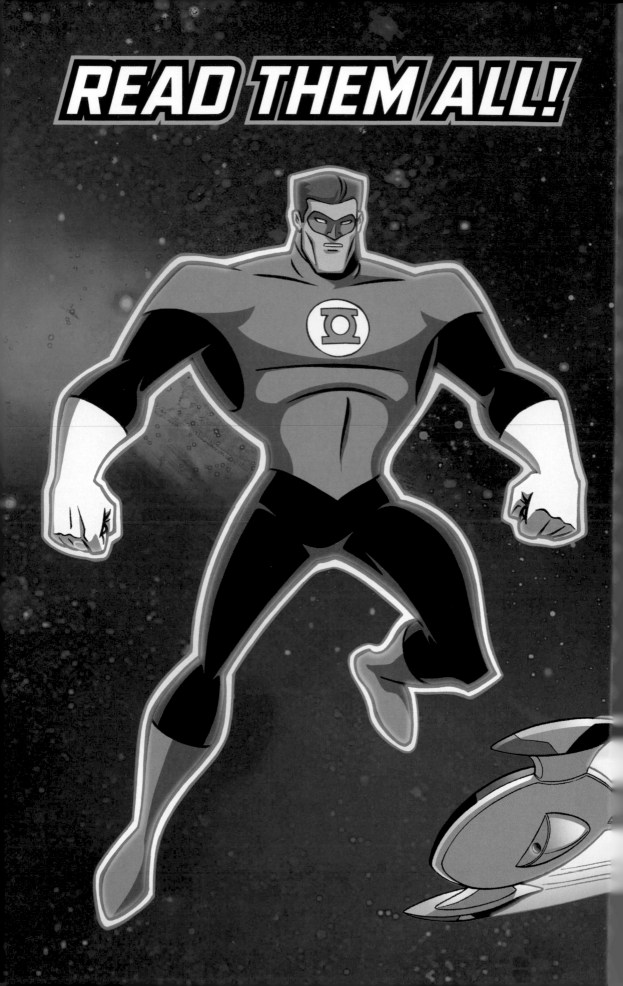

READ THEM ALL!

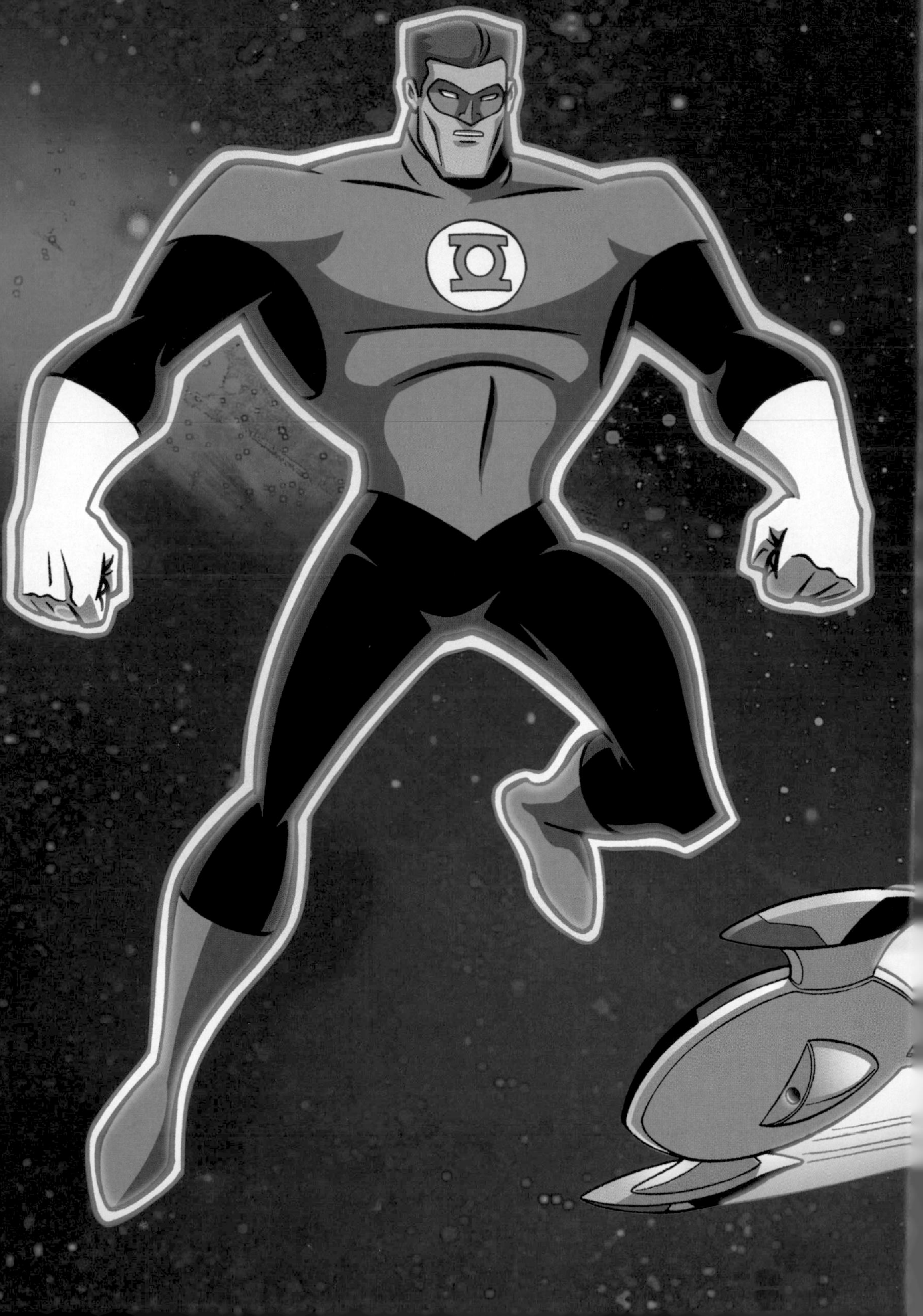

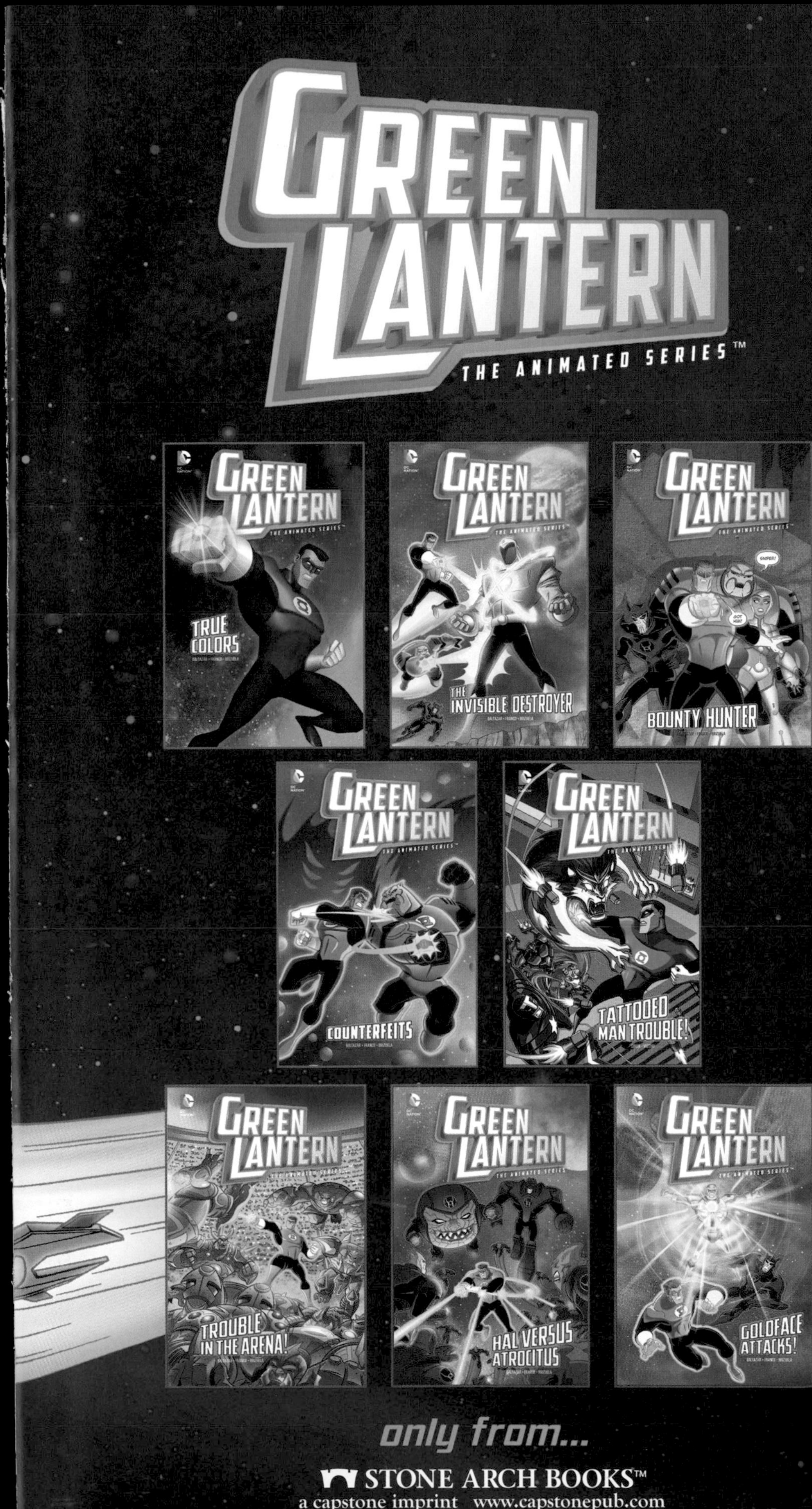
GREEN LANTERN
THE ANIMATED SERIES™
TRUE COLORS
THE INVISIBLE DESTROYER
BOUNTY HUNTER
SNIPER!
GOT HIM!
COUNTERFEITS
TATTOOED MAN TROUBLE!
TROUBLE IN THE ARENA!
HAL VERSUS ATROCITUS
GOLDFACE ATTACKS!
only from...
STONE ARCH BOOKS™
a capstone imprint www.capstonepub.com

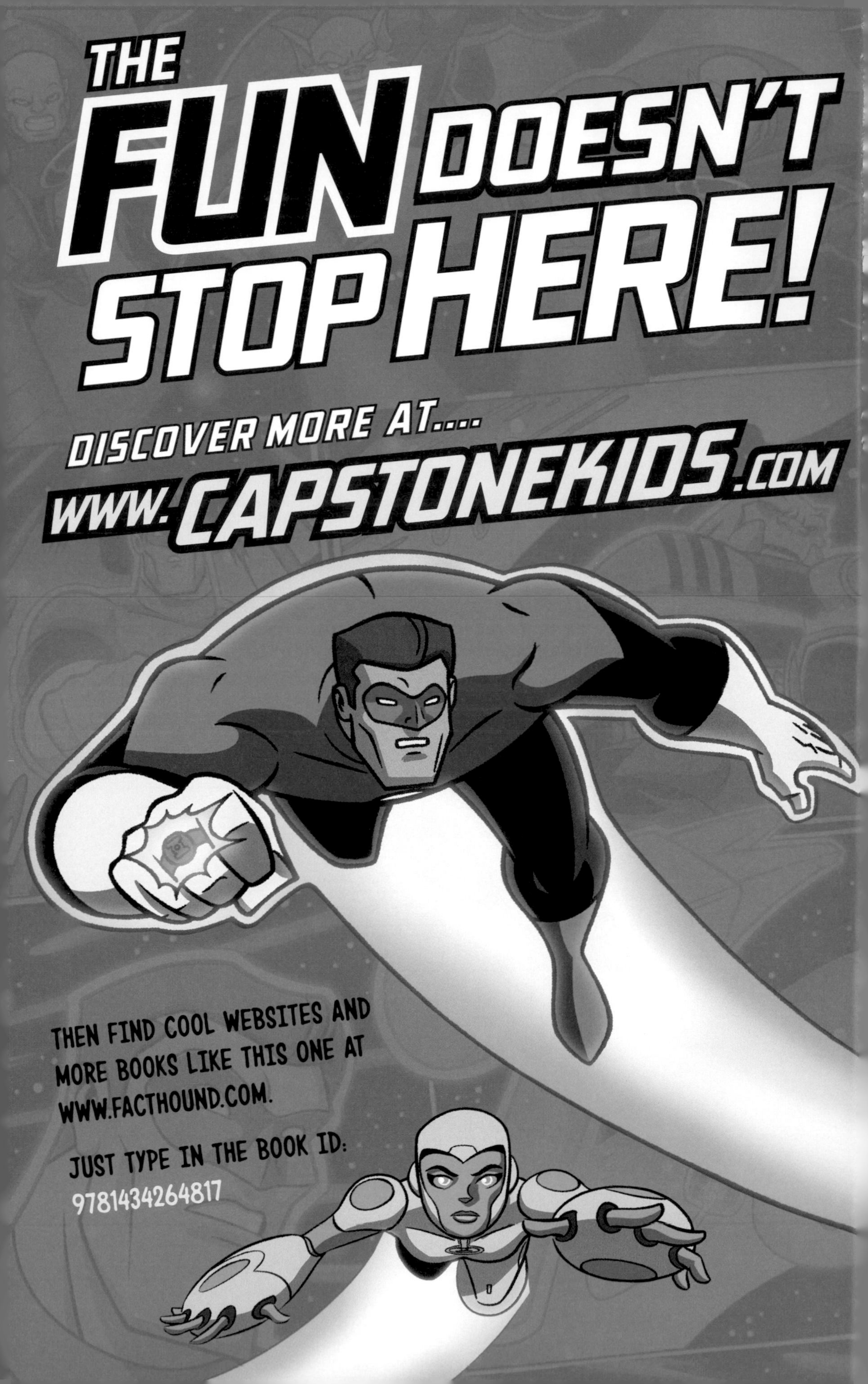
THE FUN DOESN'T STOP HERE!
DISCOVER MORE AT....
WWW.CAPSTONEKIDS.COM
THEN FIND COOL WEBSITES AND MORE BOOKS LIKE THIS ONE AT WWW.FACTHOUND.COM.
JUST TYPE IN THE BOOK ID:
9781434264817